Awakening the Virgin 2

Awakening the Virgin 2

Edited by
Nicole Foster

alyson books
los angeles

MANUFACTURED IN THE UNITED STATES OF AMERICA.

THIS TRADE PAPERBACK ORIGINAL IS PUBLISHED BY ALYSON PUBLICATIONS,
P.O. BOX 4371, LOS ANGELES, CALIFORNIA 90078-4371.
DISTRIBUTION IN THE UNITED KINGDOM BY
TURNAROUND PUBLISHER SERVICES LTD.,
UNIT 3, OLYMPIA TRADING ESTATE, COBURG ROAD, WOOD GREEN,
LONDON N22 6TZ ENGLAND.

FIRST EDITION: DECEMBER 2003

03 04 05 06 07 **a** 10 9 8 7 6 5 4 3 2 1

ISBN 1-55583-515-5

CREDITS
• "WHAT DO U LIKE?" BY ZONNA WAS ORIGINALLY PUBLISHED BY
  STORYMISTRESS.COM IN 2002.
• COVER PHOTOGRAPHY BY STACEY HALPER.

CONTENTS

INTRODUCTION:
DIEHARD VIRGIN

I've been practically swamped with letters since the first volume of *Awakening the Virgin* was released in 1998. "I'll never be able to thank you enough," wrote a woman from Jackson, Mich. "*Awakening the Virgin* got me so turned on I finally acted on my own deepest fantasies—it was either that or burst!" Well, my Midwestern friend was only one of many, because *Awakening the Virgin* is one of Alyson's best-selling lesbian erotica collections of all time.

I've decided to do things a bit differently for volume two, mainly to satisfy my best friend, Jeannie, who believes every woman has an infinite amount of virginity.

"I just lost my spanking virginity," Jeannie announced to me over the phone one hot sticky summer day. Another time—the same summer, I think—she said, "Guess what, Nicole? I just strapped on my first dildo. Wow! What a revelation. I have never felt so *virginal*."

"You felt virginal?" I said. "Then, girlfriend, it must have been good." (Jeannie's a total tart.)

I think it's cool how Jeannie always manages to explore new things. Women have multiple orgasms, so why shouldn't we have multiple virginities? In expanding the definition of "virgin" to encompass every time we gay gals dare to try something new, I was able to be more flexible with the range of these accounts. For example, Rachel Kramer Bussel's "Rock Star Spanking" tells about a first-time experience at a sex club; "Loved It and Set It Free" by Lisa

Archer is a woman's wistful memory of her first dildo; and Julie McKinley's "Rough Trade" relates the deliciously satisfying story of a spoiled brat's first hard lesson. And for you jaded types, there's Terri Giani's "Raging Hormones," in which the dyke who's done it all is seduced by her married supervisor, who's also pregnant. And, yes, those *are* the hormones she's talking about.

But rest assured, there are plenty of first-time lesbian sex stories too, such as Shar Rednour's hilarious "Behind the Propane Tank," in which Shar gets yelled at by a famous drag queen, and Karla Hodges's "The Light at the End of the Road," which tells the story of an innocent college girl who finds a wild lover in her down-the-street neighbor. Jackie Strano's revelatory coming-out story, "Dirty Laundry and Pink Champagne," is as much about looking for one's people as it is about getting laid.

I invite you to read and reread these sizzling stories. All are certain to unveil new truths each time you do. I also hope that whether you've slept with another woman or not, you always remember to keep searching for the virgin within. Of course, as soon as you find her, you'll want to lose her again. But that's the fun of it.

—Nicole Foster

Dirty Laundry and Pink Champagne

JACKIE STRANO

She was 19. I was 18. She was born and raised in Sacramento, Calif. I had lived in 10 different apartments in two different states. She had been a cheerleader in high school. I had played guitar, cut class, and gotten stoned during lunch in high school. She drove an old Mustang, and I took the bus from my mother's house. When we met I was working in the mailroom at an office building, and she was the secretary. Her hair was curly and dark, her nails long and red, and her dresses tight. I was a tomboy obsessed with Ann Wilson, the lead singer of Heart—a stone fox and rock star goddess.

We would gossip about everyone we worked with—like Jenny the Jehovah's Witness with her flaming red hair, who used to witness by displaying a copy of *Watchtower* magazine on her desk. One day it came out that she was having a torrid affair with Ben, the snack delivery guy, who told everyone that God had sent Jenny to him. They got married all of a sudden and babies soon followed. Then there was Phil, who always smelled like alcohol and told really racist jokes. I would get really pissed off in general, but also for Ben's sake, because Ben is black, but Ben told me that he liked Phil, and that they got along great, and that I shouldn't worry about it. I didn't get it. Finally, we talked about Carla. She supposedly lived with her "cousin," whom she brought to an office party once. It seems they weren't related at all, yet her "cousin" was listed as Carla's beneficiary on her life insurance policy.

But our favorite topic was music and musicians and getting out. Every Monday she heisted the calendar section of the Sunday *Chronicle* off her boss's desk so we could check out San Francisco events and bands as we sat at Dairy Queen sharing fries and slurping Mr. Mistys.

This was way before the Internet, so the calendar section was our lifeline to news about touring bands like The Pretenders, Stevie Nicks, Depeche Mode, Sisters of Mercy, the Cure, and Siouxsie and the Banshees.

We took smoke breaks together. I lit her Virginia Slims Extra Longs (in a box) before lighting the Camel Light stuck between my lips, then told her how I desperately wanted to move to San Francisco.

We felt stifled in Sacramento. The heat alone during summer oppressed us as much as the small-minded hicks that ruled the suburbs. I was a typical teenager, hating everyone and sure that no one "understood me." But she did. She made Sacramento tolerable. We would go to El Torito and order margaritas because they didn't check IDs. On Friday nights we'd do speed and go see the Dead Kennedys at K Street Mall or Joan Jett at the Oasis Ballroom, then stay up all weekend. Soon we were calling in sick on Mondays—it didn't take long for us to get fired together.

We got other jobs; me at the alternative record store and her at some other office. She finally broke up with her boyfriend and moved into a trailer park off of Madison Avenue. I met her there one day for lunch so we could do more crank in a comfortable setting. She greeted me at the door wearing a slip and some frilly spaghetti-stringed top that revealed her grown-up cleavage. "It's called a camisole," she informed me. "C'mon in. I'm ironing my shirt."

"At lunch?" I asked, but felt only too happy that she was overly concerned about creases if it meant I got to watch her iron in tiny undergarments. I tried to look nonchalant and act like her friend from work. But I was nervous and felt jittery, like a teenage boy who'd walked in on his friend's mom while she was getting dressed. We may have only been a year apart in age, but she just seemed so much more womanly. I still felt like an awkward teenager trying to figure out what to do with my hair.

I lit a cigarette and started talking about my day. Told her that Nina Hagen was coming to town and that the new 12-inch from Echo and the Bunnymen had arrived in the store from England.

She told me how her new boss was acting really skanky and trying to flirt with her and saying things that weirded her out. I told her she should talk to the labor board and call a union rep. What I wanted to do was transform into a 7-foot-tall Hell's Angel, show up at her work, kick in his door, and tell him to stay away from my woman.

How could she possibly know I was in love with her? Could she ever be in love with me? How could *I* possibly know I was in love with her? I wanted to kiss her so bad but I thought she would freak out and call me a dyke and never speak to me again. I couldn't bear the thought of living without our drunken nights of rocking out to music and me making her laugh. I couldn't bear the thought of life in that hellhole without her.

I didn't know I was in the closet because I didn't even know I was gay. I hadn't said the words to myself. I just knew I was never going to marry a man and that she was the only person who made me feel truly happy. One night we were driving around with Billy idol blaring from the tape deck. We drove to Discovery Park, a local cruise spot where partyers parked and dating teenagers did more than that. We drank some beer and threw rocks high into the air. Bats swooped down after the rocks above our heads. It was a very creepy and cool way to spend a hot summer night when you're bored out of your mind, when you think you're ready for better things.

"Hey, have you noticed that girl at J Street Café?" she asked, and proceeded to tell me about this girl she saw at a café downtown. The girl had butched-off hair and wore Birkenstocks and didn't shave her legs or her underarms. She said that the girl smiled at her and acted kind of funny.

I was appalled that she would care about anyone wearing Birkenstocks. The girl sounded like a UC Davis student, and that meant she was rich. Fuck her. I said, "Why should I care about someone like that? Why are you talking about someone in Birkenstocks?"

"I hate Birkenstocks," she laughed.

"What's the point?" I tried to control my anger and the confusion of my feelings.

"Don't you get it? I think she's a dyke."

My brain slammed shut and my ears started ringing. I wanted to grab her hair and kiss her hard. I want to throw her down in the backseat and get her pregnant. I wanted to run so far from this stupid, sweltering, festering sore of a city and never come back.

"I gotta get out of here," I growled loudly. I prided myself on what I called my "nobody's stuck" philosophy. This is America. We could do whatever we wanted. A brilliant plan formulated in my brain—the words stumbled out: "I'm joining the army so I can get the fuck outta here."

Her eyes lit up with the idea of new possibilities. "Me, too. I'll follow you."

She never ceased to amaze me. I smiled and forgot about the Birkenstocks girl.

"Will they let us do basic training together?" she asked as we got back into her Mustang.

We stopped by the River City Market to buy Andre pink champagne, Slim Jims, and Chee-tos, then headed back to her trailer.

She had this way of driving that made me feel like we were in our own movie. She held the steering wheel with her right hand and propped her other elbow up in the open window, where she balanced her cigarette between her fingers, waving them along with the melody of the song that was playing. With her long red nails and her rings, which she said were "Black Hills gold," I thought she looked European or like she belonged somewhere else, anywhere besides Sacramento. Her hair would blow around as she sang along, accenting the meaning of the words with her cigarette hand. Our conversations that night and any night were adamant, loud, deep, passionate, without so much as a word to each other except for the song's lyrics. We screamed along with the radio, barreling into the night, raging against the predetermined destinies that tried to bind us in. Iggy Pop's "Lust for Life" and "Gimme Danger" were our anthems. We blasted them from the speakers, and our lungs screamed, demanding that Fate take notice.

That night when we got to her trailer we were high with our new plans, and looking back on it, maybe she was high, too, with her lesbian conversation starter. I propped the screen door open and held our bag of Friday fun as she dug for her keys. I let my eyes travel down her back to check out her butt as she bent over to work the lock, her elbow just slightly pushing her chest up into its black lace top as she twisted the key into the fake brass doorknob. She was gorgeous. I was in love.

She tossed her curly hair over her shoulder and turned around, landing those black-lined, sparkling eyes at me to say, "Are you just gonna stand there?" and then she laughed and threw down her keys and purse.

I pretended to trip on the step as I walked through the door. I dramatically tossed the bag of goodies around in my arms like I was struggling against letting them fly out of the bag as I caught my balance supposedly just in time. She laughed at my goofiness. Even if I'd wanted to say something suave, I wouldn't have been able to spit it out. My job was to make her laugh, and she made me feel like the smartest, funniest, most talented person alive. She loved my loud jokes and extravagant tales about my big immigrant family. She also took my advice and made me feel cultured. For instance, I convinced her to let her hair dry naturally instead of the daily torture she did with the blow-dryer and hot rollers. Now her hair hung in beautiful spirals. I told her how sexy it was. (She later blunt-cut some of it and would take a crimping iron to it to make it oh-so New Wave.) I made her espresso. She'd never had it before. I bought her an espresso maker from Cost Plus Imports, and she loved it. Now we could be permanently wired.

She poured our pink champagne and I convinced her

that after the Army we would go to S.F. and go to college, because the military would pay for it. She could study photography and take pictures of bands for money. She had a visual artist's aesthetic about everything. I loved the way she looked at things and what she saw when she did. She had an intense eye for detail and could describe inanimate objects like they were people. As we finished the first bottle, the Army plan got scrapped when I realized Ronald Reagan was nobody I was going to kill for and that he would probably find some reason for war. Sometime later we all learned where the hell Grenada was, and that it was smaller than L.A. I didn't want to die just because I wanted a free ticket out of nowhere.

After my third glass of champagne—or fourth?—I felt ambitious. I started asking her about the hairy girl at the café. I'm not sure how, but a few minutes later we were fighting over whether I had insinuated that she had said something stupid. As she kicked me out, I reminded her that I didn't have any money or a car. "So unless you're planning on giving me a ride, I am staying right here and finishing my drink!"

"Oh, you can put up with me for a drink?" or something like that, she screamed sarcastically.

I guzzled my champagne and ended up storming down the road toward the main drag anyway, dramatically slamming the door behind me. A few minutes later, thank God, she was yelling after me, "Get back here and get your cigarettes and your stupid espresso maker."

Years later, when I heard the term "dyke drama," I wistfully recollected that situation, and decided that it meant a couple was spending a lot more time fighting than fucking.

I stomped back into the trailer, grabbed my cigarettes

and lighter, and turned just in time to see the espresso maker being hurled across the kitchen, slamming against the open door behind me. She obviously meant to miss me. I started laughing, took my shoes off, and frantically threw them out the door. That diffused the tension and inspired a look on her face that egged me on. "You think you're the only one who can throw shit? C'mon, let's go. Gimme your best shot." She moved toward me and pulled back her hand, I flinched a little as she reached past me to shut the door behind me. I let out a breath I hadn't realized I was holding and she laughed a little wickedly. *Good one,* I thought. She was so close to me. "More champagne?" she said and turned back to the couch.

She opened another bottle and poured us both a huge glass until the bottle was empty. Suddenly I was having a revelation. For the first time in my life I imagined what someone looked like naked, and that someone was her. *Of course.* I could lust for her, here in the same room with her, and she wouldn't even know it. I could have this fantasy in my mind without fear of retribution or rejection. She would never sense it. I felt giddy with the thought of going down on her because I had this sudden infusion of confidence—I knew that I would be really great at it. I listened to her story about a pet turtle she had when she was a little kid, but I didn't hear any words. Her mouth was moving, and I was thinking very loudly, *I want to fuck you.*

In my drunken delusion I convinced myself that she didn't have a clue how I really felt. I also never considered that she might be giving me hints, or that it simply might be fine for me to be imagining fucking her. I just assumed that would not be good despite all the time she spent with me.

Bauhaus droned on the stereo. "Mind if I change this?"

It was giving me a headache. I put on "Love You Live" by the Stones. My sudden movement across the room induced the spins. I tried to hold it together. I widened my eyes as if opening them more would stop the walls from swirling and staggering toward me. I told her I had to lie down or I was going to be sick. She pointed at her room. I stumbled in the dark and tripped over something. The next thing I knew I was facedown on her bedroom floor in a bunch of soft clothes that smelled like her. I inhaled deeply and felt an overwhelming sense of peace and relief. I was a little nauseous, but with each deep breath the spinning gradually subsided. The silky feel of her panties and camisoles against my skin made me perfectly content. I saw my destiny. I saw us rolling around on the floor making out. Her mouth, her skin, her hair, the smell of Spritz Forté, everything was soft and intoxicating.

I was hungry and powerful and aggressive.

I held her hands down and kissed and bit her neck as she moaned and writhed under me. I pulled her tits up and out of her bra to kiss and suck them with drunken adoration. I wanted to taste her. I wanted to be inside her. I whispered all this in her ear. She gasped at my words, and in barely a whisper said, "Finally." We kissed till our mouths were raw. I got lost in her hair and her smell. She pulled me to her, into her, on her, all around her. Grabbing the back of my head as she bit my neck, she gave me the perfect hickey. Definitive proof that I was officially a dyke.

I opened my eyes and saw blue sky outside the window. My head hurt and I had drool coming out of the side of my mouth. My shoes were off but my clothes were on. I squinted and squirmed a little and slowly started looking around. I couldn't find my shoes. I couldn't move fast. Matter of fact, I could barely move at all. I heard her in the kitchen, and I suddenly felt mortified. I achingly staggered up to go to the bathroom. I had to look at my neck in the mirror. Just as I reached for the bathroom door she appeared in the hallway. "You look like you need some coffee," she said in an extremely sweet and sexy voice. Her eyes shone. I unconsciously touched my neck, which felt bruised and tender.

"Thanks, uh, I have to pee," I said nervously. I quickly took the cup out of her hand then turned into the bathroom and shut the door behind me. I turned on the bad fluorescent light and pushed my face toward the mirror. I couldn't *see* a bruise, but in this flickering light I could hardly see anything. I sat on the toilet and put my head in my hands. "Please, please, tell me, did it happen?" As I grabbed my head, I begged my brain to reveal its secrets—was this a drunken fantasy? Had I fallen asleep on her? I took a deep breath, which only blurred everything more, because all I could smell was her sweet scent against my skin.

But suddenly I had another revelation. What wasn't a blur was my conviction. This is it, I said to myself. I looked at the bathroom door. I am going to walk out that door and demand that she pack up right now. *We're moving to San Francisco. Fuck all, we're going,* I would say. *We're quitting our jobs and leaving as soon as we can load up your car.* But what if...what if? No what-ifs. Tell her to call in sick, forever, right now. Pack up the records, pack up the books, the camera, the clothes, and get on the freeway. Drive the 86 miles to San Francisco and never look back. And minus a couple of details, that's pretty much what we did.

Loved It and Set It Free

LISA ARCHER

In 1985, my first dildo drifted out into the Baltimore Harbor on a broken bookshelf. I'd owned this dong for less than a day, but we'd been through a lot together. The night before I'd eased it inside myself—while my best friend pretended to be asleep next to me. Most people keep their first dildos till they rot. But I was different. I loved mine and set it free.

"The Boss" was a single piece of beige rubber shaped like a toy sword—with a handle and cross-guard. A 10-inch dong hung in place of a blade. The label on the package claimed it was "anatomically correct," but even then I knew 10 inches was a little on the long side.

I first laid eyes on The Boss when my friend Kim took me to a porn shop on East Baltimore Street. Kim was a born comic with gawky limbs and a wide, pouty mouth. The summer before our senior year, she carried bottles of Sun-In and hydrogen peroxide wherever she went. When we weren't swimming, she poured them over her head and lay in the sun.

By the time we went back to our all-girl school that fall, Kim's hair hung in clumps like bleached snakes. People said she dyed her hair orange to match our school colors—orange and green. So she dyed it green for one of the field hockey games.

Around that time, Kim and I were playing "I Never,"

one of the few games you can win through sheer inexperience and naïveté. In "I Never" players take turns confessing things they've never done. If the other player has done something you haven't, she owes you a penny. Right off, I won two cents easily because I'd never bleached my hair or dyed it green.

It took me a bit longer to come up with my third confession. Finally I said, "I've never really gotten a good look at another person's genitals."

This was true. Although I'd made out with both boys and girls, we rarely took off our clothes. Instead, we groped each other in dark, semipublic places, fumbling with buttons, bras, belt buckles, and zippers, and glancing over our shoulders every few seconds expecting our parents to catch us in the act. I'd even lost my virginity on the floor of a tool shack.

I expected Kim to question my confession, but she just nodded and tossed me another penny.

"You should come over and watch porn movies the next time my parents go away. That'll give you plenty of chances to check out other people's equipment."

Unlike my parents, the last in town to buy a microwave or any new appliance, Kim's family owned a VCR. Whenever her mom and dad went out of town, Kim rented porn. We planned our private video screening months in advance and waited for her folks' next vacation.

Kim got her videos from a seedy shop on "The Block," the 400 block of East Baltimore Street that makes up Baltimore's red-light district. Growing up in the sub-suburban sprawl of Baltimore County, I'd never been to The Block—until one night when Kim borrowed her mom's Honda Civic.

"That's it." Kim pointed out the window. "Look now, or you'll miss it."

I pressed my face against the passenger window. Neon lights danced against the starless sky, then we dove back into the night.

"Was that it?"

"Yeah. It's only one block. I'll go around again."

The second time, she coasted along more slowly so I could read the signs:

GOLDEN NUGGET LOUNGE

THE CRYSTAL PUSSYCAT

GRESSER'S GAYETY LIQUORS

SAVETTA'S PSYCHIC READINGS

CRAZY JOHN'S

THE PLAZA SALOON

Glamorous names for kids growing up in Baltimore.

We didn't rent any videos that night. But Kim pointed out Sylvester's, the store where she rented porn. "They have booths in the back where you can watch videos, but you don't want to go in there. The walls are sticky and gross. Let's just wait till my parents go away, and we'll rent a few."

Finally Kim's parents scheduled an overnight camping trip. All day at school on the Friday that they left, my heart and stomach fluttered. After our last class, Kim and I met in the locker room and changed out of our school uniforms into jeans.

"Hurry up," said Kim. "I want to get down to The Block while it's still light out, so no one will break into my mom's car." We slung our backpacks over our shoulders and walked out.

As we drove the little Honda downtown, I pressed my face against the window and marveled at the dirt on the streets. Where I come from, dirt is brown like mud or red like sandstone. In the city, black grit cakes under your fingernails and sticks to the concrete. The wind writes messages on the sidewalk with black dust and dead leaves.

I soon realized we were driving in circles, passing the same buildings.

"Are we lost?"

"No, I'm looking for parking."

"Where are we?"

"The Block, silly."

I winced. "It looks different during the day."

While night had hidden everything but the neon signs, the sun exposed gray concrete buildings and trash piled up in the street. The neon signs looked like pale plastic tubing and dusty electrical cords.

The door to Sylvester's Videos was covered with chipped paint, faded posters, and random thumbtacks. At night I had found the place intimidating, but seeing it in the daylight was like watching a flashy porn star sleep in her underwear and snore.

Kim found a tiny parking space. She cranked her steering wheel all the way to the right and backed in fast. As her rear tires rammed the curb, her elbow struck the horn with a loud honk. Across the street, the door to Sylvester's creaked open and a guy with beady eyes and slicked-back gray hair stepped out and glared at us.

"Shit, Kim. Let's get out of here."

"No, come on."

When we crossed the street to the storefront, Kim hoisted the door open to reveal a heavy black plastic curtain. Glancing at me, she pulled aside the curtain and slipped inside. I followed her into a dimly lit square room. Videos lined the walls floor to ceiling.

The same beady-eyed man sat behind a cash register. He showed his crooked yellow teeth.

"Howdy, girls."

At the sound of his voice, two customers in the front room turned and peered at us. Both were bent over videos, with their collars turned up and hats pulled down over their eyes. Kim and I were the only two women in the store.

Kim took me on a tour of the narrow rooms with low ceilings and X-rated videos on the walls:

The Penile Colony
Hannah Does Her Sisters
Astropussy Strikes Back
Public Enema Number 1
Public Enema Number 2
Public Enema Number 3

"The booths are in the back." Kim pointed to a man who was busy slipping behind a black plastic curtain. "You can rent your video, close the curtain, pop your video in the slot, and jerk off. Lisa... Lisa!" She poked me.

I had frozen, facing a wall of rubber penises and sundry other body parts, including vulvas, hands, and arms. For the first time in my life, I could look at someone's "genitals" without worrying what the person attached to it thought of me. I didn't really think about the fact that nobody's parts really look like these creations—propped on shelves, strapped onto harnesses, packaged in plastic, hanging from hooks on walls like the cheapest toys at Toys R Us. Through my entire childhood, I had been looking at Ken dolls without dicks and Barbies without pussies. Suddenly I was looking at the opposite: dicks and pussies without bodies. What an idea.

"Haven't you ever seen a dildo before?" asked Kim.

"N-no."

"Check this out." She pointed to a plastic package containing a foot-long rubber forearm with the hand clenched in a fist. It looked like one of those dismembered arms you find in Walgreen's at Halloween.

"What do you think you're supposed to do with this?" Kim asked. "Bonk somebody over the head?"

Before I could say anything, she yanked the plastic package off the hook and bonked me over the head with it.

"Kim! Stop!"

She clasped her hands over her mouth and burst into giggles, shoulders shaking uncontrollably. Customers in the store turned and stared.

"You're going to get us kicked out of here!"

"Look. Here's the description." We huddled over the package to read the label in excited whispers:

12.5 inches long, 3 inches wide, 9 inches around
Size: Huge
Product Category: anal stimulation
Color: Black
Made of: rubber
For use in this part of the body: anus

"It's for the... the... anus?" I asked in disbelief.

"That's the butt," she whispered smugly.

"I know what an anus is, but I don't see how it could fit."

She shrugged. "Don't ask me."

"Do all these things go up your butt?" I gestured to the wall of dildos and other funny-shaped objects.

"They don't go up my butt," she giggled. "But you can put dildos up your vagina. Haven't you ever put vegetables up there?"

"No. Have you?"

"Of course."

"You're kidding. What kind?"

"Cucumbers, carrots, and zucchini. When I was younger, I used to sneak them out of the crisper and put them back when I was done."

"Ew! Yuck!"

Kim returned the rubber arm to its hook. "We're not getting this," she whispered. "Let's get some dildos. Here's a thin one. It's 8.99."

Kim handed me a package. I stared at the label. *The Boss: Anatomically Correct Dong.*

"Are you suggesting I buy this?"

"Why not? I'll buy one too."

"How do you know it'll fit?"

"You just have to try your luck. You can't try it on in a dressing room like a pair of jeans."

I laughed nervously.

"Come on," she said. "Let's move on to the videos."

I followed her back into the front room, where we rifled through hundreds of video boxes and decided on two orgy movies: *Farm Family Free for All* and *Group Grope 9.*

Growing up in the '70s, I was familiar with the made-for-TV *Roman Orgy*—where toga-clad patricians get it on with priestesses of Isis in Roman baths that look like contemporary Jacuzzis. My parents allowed me to watch these programs due to their so-called historical significance.

Perhaps I was supposed to think, *My God, how decadent!* and conclude that rampant orgies caused the fall of Rome. But instead I wondered, *Why don't people do that anymore?* I also thought "Roman orgies," like "Egyptian mummies," were ancient history. *Farm Family Free for All* and *Group Grope 9* were my first signs that the orgy lived on, at least in contemporary porn.

After hours of X-rated shopping, Kim and I finally carried our lurid wares to the cashier and spread them out on the counter. The beady-eyed man winked at us.

"You want some KY Jelly for those dongs?"

"That's not a bad idea," said Kim. "We'll take some."

Outside, dusk had fallen, and the neon signs flickered in orange, pink, and green. As we drove back to Kim's house, I shivered when a cop car whizzed by. What if they pulled us over? I pictured our head shots on the front page with a photo of The Boss underneath.

When we finally made it back to Kim's, we emptied our bags on the living room rug and tore open our dildo packages.

"Hey, The Boss doesn't have balls!" I exclaimed.

"You'll see them in the movies," said Kim. "On guard!" She held the dildo by its sword-like handle and brandished it like Excaliber. But the rubber weenie just flopped around.

I giggled. "That's one lame weapon."

"Oh, well. Let's watch the videos." Kim switched on the TV and took the videos out of their plastic boxes.

We unzipped our sleeping bags and curled up side by side, propping our heads up on pillows so we could see the TV. Punching buttons on the remote control, Kim fast-forwarded to the opening scene, where a hottie with a blond mullet and ample cleavage skipped through a cornfield in a low-cut blue gingham dress. The scene changed to the inside of a barn, where two men in plaid flannel shirts and overalls were milking cows. The younger man stood up and stretched.

"Gee, Paw," he drawled. "Ah wish Sissy would git here with those vittles. Ah need a break."

Outside, the blond in blue gingham peeked through a crack in the barn door. Seeing the men, she slipped one hand up her gingham skirt and opened the door.

"Did Ah hear y'all say yuh need some refreshments?"

The men turned and gaped as she stepped into the barn, toting a straw basket in the crook of her arm and fondling her breasts.

I shook my head. "God, can you believe these accents? Nobody talks like that."

"Watch this." Kim pointed the remote and the video flew into fast-forward. Six people in plaid, flannel, calico, and gingham speed-walked into the barn, tore off one another's clothes, sprawled on the hay, and plugged themselves into one another's orifices, fucking and sucking as fast as an assembly line.

"Damn it, Kim, I can't see any genitals!" I grabbed the remote control and pushed "Play." My jaw dropped. Two tanned, tight-bodied girls locked in a 69 were licking each other. With their identical-size big boobs and blond mullets, they looked like twins. In fact, they were supposed to be twins. This was *Farm Family Free for All*. My heart beat faster. I'd never seen two girls having sex, even on screen. Out of the corner of my eye, I peered at Kim. Did she know this was going to be in the video? I knew orgies meant sex scenes with more than one man, more than one woman, or several of both—but somehow it had never dawned on me that I'd be watching women have sex with each other. Nor had I anticipated my response.

I gaped at the screen, transfixed, my crotch tingling under the covers. I fidgeted, crossing my legs, squeezing my thighs together. Finally, when I couldn't stand it anymore, I slipped my hands under the blankets. Kim's elbow brushed against mine, so the tiny hairs on our arms stood on end. She was doing the same thing I was, but I didn't dare look at her. I wondered if the people we knew would be able to tell we'd watched lesbian porn. Would they see it in our eyes?

In English class earlier that year we had been talking about Virginia Woolf. The class had been sitting in a semi-circle around the edge of the room, facing our teacher Mrs. Byrd. My mind had been wandering, when suddenly someone had mentioned the word *lesbian*.

A girl named Patty had raised her hand. "Have there ever been any lesbians in our school?"

"Yes," said Mrs. Byrd. "We've had some."

"How can you tell?"

"Sometimes two girls are...closer than normal."

"Does the school do anything about it?" asked Patty.

"We try to split them up," said Mrs. Byrd. "Sometimes we tell their parents."

A hush fell over the room as we all exchanged nervous glances. I looked at Kim, who sat across the room from me doodling. She didn't look up.

If they found out, would they separate us? Tell our parents?

Meanwhile, on *Farm Family Free For All*, the rest of the family was joining the girls with mullets. The scene turned into a more traditional orgy, with barely differentiated writhing bodies—just one monster with multiple arms and legs. I circled my clit with my fingertip, less interested in the family scene. But I couldn't admit—even to myself—the girl-on-girl porn had turned me on.

Kim grunted next to me. She was snoring.

"Come on, I know you're not really asleep."

No answer.

"Kim?" I put my hand on her shoulder.

Maybe she was really asleep. I thought about waking her up, then changed my mind and circled my clit faster, feeling lucky and slightly out-of-control. My back tensed, my heart quickened, and I tried not to make any noise or move anything except my hand. I had played this game before. The goal was to come without waking the other person. Sometimes, of course, the other person woke up and just pretended to still be sleeping. I had faked a deep slumber myself when someone was masturbating beside me.

Next to me, Kim took slack-jawed, measured breaths. She was either out like a light or damn good at pretending. Her legs twitched under the covers. I groped around on the cold floor for my dong. My fingers, wet with juice, slid over the rubber—solid, cold, and veiny—and I pulled it under the covers. It rested hard against my thigh. Slowly, I maneuvered its cold head against the wet lips of my cunt. Circling my clit, I rubbed the head on my swollen, tender pussy lips. My back and ass tensed; I was really close.

I took a deep breath and tried to ease the cock inside me. It didn't fit. I pushed, took a deep breath, and pushed again—still, no go. Suddenly I remembered the KY Jelly. I reached my hand out from under the blanket and felt around on the floor. It was still in the bag. I tore the box open and squeezed a glob of clear, cold gel into my palm.

I couldn't believe how cold it was. I thought of Kim's refrigerated cucumbers. I didn't want anything that cold near my pussy, but if I wanted to get The Boss inside, I knew I'd have to brave that lube.

I covered the head of the dildo in KY. Then, with a deep breath, I squeezed the tube directly into my vagina. The lube spilled onto the sleeping bag and spread in a cold puddle under my butt. I shivered and glanced at Kim. Her eyes were still closed. I took a deep breath and pushed the dildo inside me. It filled my cunt—stretched me so much I burned like a ball of fire. I shook uncontrollably; I was really turned on. I looked at Kim again. I craned my neck and brushed my lips against her cheek. I reached out the tip of my tongue and licked her hair.

Kim stirred and turned over on her side. I froze. I listened for her breath. I was sure she was awake, but by then I couldn't stop. I eased the dildo in and out of my cunt. The woman on the screen was coming like a swimmer gasping for air. The man squeezed his cock and came too. I came with them, melting into the scene: The cock inside me was his cock. My sounds shot out of her mouth. My wave of pleasure rocked her body on the screen. My cunt contracted and spit out the dildo, which lay wet between my thighs. Warmth spread through my stomach, heart, and limbs. I sank into the floor.

Someone nudged me.

"Stop it," I murmured.

"Wake up."

"What? What time is it?"

"5:30."

"What the fuck?" I glanced around the dark, unfamiliar room.

"Wake up." Kim's shadowy form bent over me.

I suddenly remembered where I was.

"Lisa, listen to me. We have to get rid of these now."

"Get rid of what?"

"These." She bumped me on the cheek with something rubber, then walked over to the doorway to switch on the lights. I winced as they blinked on. What was she talking about? Jesus, what did I do last night? I remembered the wall of dildos, The Boss, and licking Kim's hair. *Shit!* I thought. *Was she awake when I did that? What does she think of me?*

"Lisa!" Kim repeated, bonking me on the head. "We've got to get rid of these things before my parents get home. They'll be back early this morning."

"We can't just throw them away. They're not cheap."

"Do you want to take them home with you?"

"Uh, no." I peered at the dildos as my eyes adjusted to the light. "I don't think I can."

"What should we do with them then? We can't just throw them in the trash, or bury them in the backyard. The dogs'll get at them."

"Can we burn them?"

"God, no! They'd stink."

"Well, then, let's just walk a few blocks down the street and throw them in someone else's trash."

"Good idea. We can take the car and drive a little ways away. We'll take the videos back to the store too." She put the VCR on rewind.

It was still dark outside. The crickets were chirping as we stepped out into the cold, wet air. Kim drove while I dozed in the passenger seat with the dildos in my lap, wrapped in newspaper. The car screeched to a stop.

"Where are we?" The sky had turned dark blue. I rolled down my window, tasting the salt air.

"We're at Fell's Point. I was thinking we could throw them in the water," said Kim. We climbed out of the car. I followed her to the edge of the pier. Water lapped at the dock, and the seabirds squawked and flapped their wings. One swooped within inches of the water, a white ghost.

Holding my bundle of newspaper and the dildos, I peered down into the black water.

"It's a shame to let these sink to the bottom of the harbor."

"I know! Let's float them out to sea on one of those boards over there." Kim darted away and came back seconds later, dragging a broken bookcase. She pulled off the top shelf and dislodged several long, rusty nails.

"We'll put them on a raft. That way, someone might find them."

We lowered the board into the water. Kim tore off a sheet of newspaper and wrote:

S.O.S.
FREE TO A GOOD HOME

I placed the dildos side by side. Wrapped in newsprint, they looked like twins in swaddling clothes. I thought of Romulus and Remus, the twins abandoned to the elements, who washed up onshore and founded Rome. Who knew what great fortune or conquest lay in store for our dildos? Would they be suckled by she-wolves? I watched them float away, convinced that some lonely soul, who desperately needed dildos, would find them.

Stockings

JENNY KIRKPATRICK

The first time I had an honest sexual experience had little to do with realizing I was a lesbian or with becoming sober. It happened at a shoe store. I'm just going to tell you, and I hope you let go of your prejudices about shoes and read the whole story.

I was 23 and had moved to St. Louis because there was a job opening for office manager at the Fashion Merchandising and Design School. I couldn't afford to go there, so I thought, *Hey, maybe this way I can take a class now and then at a discount.* So I got an apartment on the west end and was having my first little-city experiences.

I got very caught up in wearing the right thing. Impressing the gay boys and my inner Joan Rivers. Lucky for me my best friend was a hairdresser, so at least that part was taken care of. I had auburn hair down to my chin, a bit longer in front than in the back. Supercool bangs, chopped straight across, accented my green eyes to the hilt. (Thank you, David.) I clumped it up with product and it smelled great, if I say so myself. It didn't take long for working downtown to bore me, so I kind of started acting like I was in a movie, *starring* as a girl who worked downtown. I bought a pink fitted suit from Frederick's of Hollywood, complete with miniskirt, of course. I stocked up on thigh-high stockings and camisoles. I had a few push-up bras to help Mother Nature. If I had to wear office attire, at least I would have something luxurious on underneath!

I have to mention that I was soooo horny and hard up. All my friends were guys or straight girls. No one seemed to be interested in me that way. And, frankly, the dykes my friends introduced me to were all either married (at least for the moment), or going through a breakup longer than their "marriage," or not worth dating at all. I took to masturbating in the women's room. I would scoot up my skirt and push my hand in between my sweaty thighs (when you're at a desk typing all day, your legs together, swathed in polyester or some form of nonnatural fibers, they get sweaty).

The heat from my pussy would convert the stall into a steam room. The idea of others walking in terrified me but also turned me on so much I could come in record time.

I jacked my clit furiously. My hand a blur, my nails biting into my flesh, until I came, jerking my moans into my lungs like a drunk trying to hide the hiccups. Later in the afternoon, I enjoyed the juices running down my leg, warming me and reminding me of my naughty "coffee break."

I enjoyed my little downtown pretend life. I read detective novels from the library at lunch. Treated myself to a fancy coffee drink on Wednesdays.

One particular Wednesday, with my whipped-cream-topped treat in hand I wandered into Shooze, a smallish store with a wall of shoes and clever, animal-print round racks displaying them. Shooze also sold random hip accessories like striped stockings, velvet studded wristbands, and fishnet dresses. I was wearing my pink suit and felt just a little embarrassed that I looked so officey—it took me years to realize that no one in real life wears a Frederick's suit to the office. I kind of wanted whoever might be in this righteous store to know I was really a dyke with my own studded wristbands at home. But I didn't worry about it too much. It was this outfit I needed shoes for anyway. When I bought the suit I couldn't afford to get the right pair, so I was embarrassingly forced into coupling the suit with these cream pumps my cousin had demanded I get for her wedding.

No one was in the store. This sort of place was usually closer to a college or in the mall.

"May I help you?" a voice said. I turned to see a very cute woman who I immediately wanted. She had brown hair, short around her face—the color of a perfect milk chocolate bar, and it was shiny and tousled. She wore brown vintage men's pants hanging loose on her hips, and a men's undershirt, white against her tan arms, with a black bra underneath. I noticed a little horn on a strip of leather around her neck.

"Yes, I need a pair of white or pink high heels to go with this suit. I'm a..."

"Size 8," she said with me.

"Yes, you can tell that?" I smiled, glad my lip gloss had been freshly applied.

"I love my job," she said simply. "Sit here. I'll take care of you."

I sat in a leopard-print '60s-era chair, noticing for the first time that my skirt barely reached the top of my thigh-high stockings.

"I think you might find these to your liking," she said, returning from behind a zebra curtain.

"Shall I just set this here?" I referred to my coffee drink.

"I can take it for you." She looked down. "Whipped cream? Right on."

Yikes, I hoped I didn't have whipped cream on my lips. I licked them to confirm that raspberry was all I could taste. "Dessert in a cup," I replied.

She put some boxes on the floor, then hitched her pant leg up just a bit before kneeling down on one knee. Her eyes were level with my thighs.

I bent over to take off my pump but she wagged a finger between us, "No, no, no, no. That's for me to do." She cupped that place where the ankle meets the heel with one hand. I must have been frozen, because she did a gentle shake and said, "Relax, I've got you," before she slipped my shoe off. I think I groaned. I sank further into my chair, unconsciously sliding my pelvis closer to her. She wrapped her warm hand around my foot and held me there as she opened a box with one hand and pulled out a white heel that had almost nothing to it. My chest noticeably rose and fell with increased desire. My nerves flamed from her touch.

I'd worn sheer black stockings that revealed my red toe-nail polish. Her hand returned to the place behind my ankle and eased my foot past the thin straps of the vamp. "Voilà." She looked to my face for approval.

I had to shake my head just a bit to get out of my trance. I looked at my foot. A single pearl-colored textured strap held my toes and another slunk up diagonally past my arch to the outside of my foot.

"Is that, uh, snakeskin?" I was trying to say something shoe-store-like. I couldn't believe I was so out of control, so quickly and so, so...*at a shoe store!*

"Alligator. But no gator died for this amount, right?" She laughed.

"Right. I mean it is little. Not that I mind killing alligators. I mean, I haven't done that, I'm, I'm not a gator killer." I stuttered then laughed. "OK, there's not a lot to it, is there?"

"You like to leave more to the imagination?" she said, but not to my face. Her brown eyes traveled up my legs to my thighs. A surge of blood swelled my clit so fast I had to part my legs a little to fit it. My nipples became bullets pushing into the helpful padding of my bra. I squirmed just enough to show the lacy tops of my stockings.

My saleswoman-lust-dyke brought her big eyes to mine, waiting for my answer.

"Yes," I whispered. "Sometimes."

She placed her strong hand behind my knee and slipped the shoe off with the other hand. *Why would you need to touch that high to pull off a shoe?* I thought. *Have I just been horny too long? Was this in my imagination?* I have been much less aroused by a drunken lesbian grappling at my crotch than by this woman simply wrapping her warm fingers around my heel.

"Let's try another one, OK?" she asked.

"The other one," I said quickly between tense breaths.

Her eyebrow went up in question. "Ah, your partner here is feeling ignored?"

"Yes, you know, you can't just do one side. I mean, not to tell you how to do it or anything."

"No offense taken. How would I know unless you tell me?"

I grinned and looked down. I had a moment then where I took conscious control over my fumbling desire. What did I have to lose, after all? A shoe store? If I let myself be swept up in passion and I was all wrong, I could still just walk out of here and never see her again, so who cared? I mean, I was sitting there wearing my Frederick's, after all. Why did I get it? Just to jack off in the bathroom? Well, yeah, actually, but hey, why not share the wealth?

"Here, you might like this better." Going to my other foot, she tilted my leg to the outside so my thighs parted even more. I could felt the cool air hit my pussy as that last inch of steamy skin separated. I remembered my fun in the ladies room earlier and knew my special smell must be easing toward her. She leaned in directly between my legs. I gasped, and she leaned back with a shoe spoon.

"Sorry, I dropped this. I need to use a tool for this lovely specimen."

"I see." I gripped the arms of my chair and edged my cunt forward. "Are you sure you need to use that? I prefer your hands to the plastic."

I could see down her shirt just enough to keep me curious. I watched the muscles of her tanned arm as she moved the box closer. Mostly I felt her hand on my foot. I remembered all the friends who thought it odd that I would massage my feet at home for hours, then go to my vibrator. I finally stopped letting people know about the shoe photo shoots I'd done—just sneaking a downward pic now and then at special events. And now, it was all making sense.

She slipped on a pump that covered my heel and had an ultra pointed toe à la 1965. It gave me toe cleavage.

"What do you think?" She again put a hand behind my knee, then lifted my foot up a little more as if to show off a gem—getting it into better light—then lowered it again. Her hand didn't leave me though as she began to press a finger into my arch, a tight squeeze between my skin and the leather bottom. I gasped.

She looked me directly in the eye as she slid her other hand up the inside of my thigh. "Do you like that?"

"Yes," I panted.

"Do you want more?"

"Yes." With no pretense I slid all the way down on the seat and spread my legs open. My skirt hiked up on its own with the movement. My clit bulged against my pink thong.

She barely even moved, pressing her mouth into me and sucking my swollen girl-knob, marrying her wet mouth with my wet cunt. She rolled my stocking down so my foot was free. Pulling from my hotness, she brought her mouth to my precious footsie and covered it with kisses, then sucked on each and every toe.

I gasped and squirmed and tried to stifle my screams, vaguely thinking there might be another worker or customer somewhere. "Oh, my God, this has never, ahhh, oh, oh, you," I breathed, "you're my—"

"Shhh. You have the most beautiful feet I've ever seen. Your toes are perfect and so edible. I can't believe how amazing you are."

"Oh, God." I hung my head back, letting my hair swing and letting the pleasure consume me, no longer worried what anyone else thought. My dyke-foot-goddess pushed her fingers into me while still holding my foot and eating and sucking and biting at me. I jammed my pussy into her hand and ripped open my shirt to get at my tits. With one motion, my bra sprung open from its front clasp. My nipples ached from being constrained for so long. I barely brushed my fingers over them for an electric jolt.

She looked at me as if she knew everything about me, as if she could read my mind. She could. "Oh, please, please." My pussy swelled so much I thought my skin would burst.

Cunt juice poured down onto the leopard-print seat. I wanted to jerk my foot away from her, because I didn't know if I could take it anymore. I didn't know if I was going to die or explode or both.

I tensed forward, clutching the chair, then my orgasm spilled forth, with me squealing and moaning as my head flew back and my chest opened. She grabbed the outside of my thighs and slammed my pussy into her mouth. I jerked her by the hair, grinding harder and harder as I came and came and came. When my screams got too loud, she shoved a shoe in my mouth, but never missed a lick as she did it.

"What's your name?"

"Karla. Yours?"

"Jenny."

"Get back here, Jenny. I'm locking the doors." Karla led me and my wobbling thighs and throbbing cunt to the back of the store, where the racks of shoes loomed over us. "This will do." We fucked all afternoon in the back, while I enjoyed the occasional taste of leather in my mouth and a sharp spike on my tongue. I shocked her when I fucked myself with the heel of a stiletto while I banged the ball of the shoe into my clit. We finally collapsed, but only after I straddled her foot, rubbing my pussy back and forth on the vintage men's shoes she was wearing while she jacked off above me.

Newly inspired, I left St. Louis a few months later to work for a shoe designer in New York's garment district. Occasionally, my boss comments on how I never complain about working overtime. I simply tell her, "I love my job."

What Do U Like?

ZONNA

DrkAngl65: What do U like?
Redbotmgrrl: everything...
DrkAngl65: What R U wearing?
Redbotmgrrl: nothing but a smile :-)
DrkAngl65: Sounds good. Can I cum over?
Redbotmgrrl: hurry or i'll start without u
DrkAngl65: [drooling] Can I watch?
Redbotmgrrl: [hand dips below desk...]

We'd been flirting online for about three months, starting off with polite small talk about where we lived and what chat rooms we'd been to, then drifting away from that and down the twisting, turning path of desire. Each session grew increasingly more graphic until we reached the point where there was nothing to be vague or unclear about. We wrote exclusively about sex. What we liked and didn't like. Preferences. Favorite positions. Erogenous zones. Fantasies. Hall of Fame encounters. Meanwhile, our fingers did the walking, and not just on the keyboard. We gave each other explicit instructions to memorize in case we ever met in person.

And then we did.

Who thought that would ever happen? Sure, I'd envisioned it a hundred times, but it was just a fantasy: She comes for a visit. We're sitting on the couch. We pick up on a recent E-mail thread and continue it in person. I'd try to be a good host and offer her something to drink. Her hand would close over mine as I handed her the glass. Our eyes would meet, and we'd exchange that magical look, the one that says, *Yeah, I'm interested—so what are you gonna do about it?*

The reality came pretty close.

She showed up at my apartment around 10 in the morning. She was early, and I had just stepped out of the shower when I heard the doorbell. I threw on a pair of jeans and a sweatshirt and ran downstairs. There she was in my doorway, looking every bit as scrumptious as her jpeg. She was shorter than I'd imagined, only 5-2 or so, but she was solidly built, with strong arms and shoulders and a curvy body she hid under loose-fitting clothes. She laughed at my wet head and we settled in on the couch to get to know each other. I put on a CD I thought she'd enjoy, then we fell into an easy conversation. I liked the sound of her voice. It was sort of low and a little raspy. The kind of voice that sounds good when it whispers things in your ear.

After a few minutes, she asked if I'd like her to brush the tangles out of my still-dripping hair. I thought that was a lovely idea and told her so. As I mounted the stairs to get my brush, she followed me. My pulse raced as we climbed closer to the bedroom. Once there, I handed her my hairbrush and she instructed me to sit on the bed. She knelt behind me on the mattress and began to brush. It felt marvelous. We chatted about this and that and nothing in particular. She told me how pretty she thought my hair was and how I looked even cuter in person than my picture. My ears grew hot as the color rose to my face. She laughed, "You look so sexy when you blush." That only made me turn a darker shade of red. She hesitated, then leaned in close.

"I wonder what it would take to get your ass to match the color of your cheeks."

My heart jumped. This was a trail we'd wandered down many times in our E-mails. We both had an overwhelming interest in B&D, although I had never explored it any further than the depth of my imagination. She, on the other hand, was well versed in the language of ropes and paddles. It was strangely exciting to hear her voice speaking the words we'd so far only written. I felt the warmth spread from my face to my cunt as she lightly kissed my neck, right below the ear. Her hands caressed my breasts through my sweatshirt, making my nipples leap to attention. Then her hands were underneath, tugging the shirt off over my head. I started to turn to embrace her, but she instructed me not to move. I sat on the bed, shivering with lust as she continued to play with my breasts, her arms reaching around from behind me.

"Stand up," she commanded.

I rose on shaky legs. Her fingers fumbled with the zipper on my jeans, sliding it down slowly as I watched. I thought of how pleased she would be to discover my wetness. She slipped my pants down to my ankles, then ordered me to kick them off. I did as I was told. As I stood there, naked in front of this virtual stranger, I felt her eyes wash over my body from head to toe.

"Open up for me," she requested, her hand sliding between my thighs.

I spread my legs as far apart as I could manage without

losing my balance. I felt her hand cup my pussy and rub it roughly for a moment. Her touch started a fire between my legs. Oh, it was hot! I was burning for her to touch me again, but she didn't appear to be in much of a hurry. Instead, she grabbed my wrists and pulled them behind my back, tying them together with a silk scarf she must have had hidden away in her pocket. Next her hands crept back to my breasts, but this time her fingers closed tightly on my nipples, pinching them hard enough to make me gasp.

"That's it," she cooed. "Let me hear how it feels."

She pinched me again and I moaned. I felt the heat of her body as it pressed up against my back.

"Lean over the bureau," she instructed.

I bent at the waist and lay my breasts atop the shiny walnut dresser. It was just a little too high, so I had to stand on my toes. I felt the cool air on my ass and cunt as I stood there, spread wide for her inspection.

"Don't move."

I heard her jump off the bed and leave the room. I was so turned on I could feel my juices run down my thigh. It tickled. I wanted desperately to wipe it away, but I didn't dare move a muscle. I wondered where she'd gone. I wondered if she was really going to spank me. With what? I assumed the hairbrush. Would it hurt? I had tried it on myself once after a particularly steamy chat we'd had online. I hadn't been able to wield it with any force, so it felt disappointingly dull. I was sure she'd have a better angle though, and I trembled as I imagined its sting.

Time ticked by. She turned up the volume on the stereo so I couldn't hear her moving around downstairs. I had no idea where she was until I felt her hand caress my ass. I jumped, startled, and she chuckled softly.

"Nervous?"

"Yes," I admitted.

"Good." I heard the smile in her voice. "I brought you a surprise. Would you like to see it?"

"Yes."

"Yes, what?"

Yes, what? I tried to remember our conversations. Yes, ma'am? Yes, please? What if I chose the wrong one? I decided to play it safe. "Yes, please, ma'am."

"You remembered. That's very good." She stroked my hair. "Look what I've brought for us to play with." She slid a black leather-coated paddle onto the bureau in my line of sight. It looked heavy. I felt faint for a moment as I imagined it connecting with my flesh. Distracted, I forgot to thank her.

"Don't you have anything to say to me?" She sounded disappointed.

"Oh... Forgive me, ma'am. Please. And thank you." I hoped it wasn't too little too late.

She sighed. "That's gonna cost you. But we'll save your punishment for later. First, we'll concentrate on pleasure."

I quivered with anticipation and braced myself for what I knew must come next. With a swoosh, the paddle landed on my ass. At first, I felt nothing, then a stinging warmth spread outward in a circle from the point of impact. Oh, it was exquisite! She hit me again and again, each time aiming for the same general area, until I felt the heat rise. Now I had two fires to worry about: my ass, which was ablaze from the spanking, and my cunt, which was melting with desire. As she continued, I grew more and more aroused. I began to grunt with each smack, which seemed to excite her.

Just when I thought I would have to beg her to stop, she

sensed I was approaching a threshold and she shifted gears. She sank to her knees and kissed and licked my sore ass, letting her tongue tease the opening to my cunt more than once. I trembled with need, and I knew she could see how wet I was as she soothed me.

"Thank you, ma'am," I remembered to say.

She seemed pleased. "You're welcome. Did that feel as good as you'd imagined?"

"Oh, yes, ma'am. Better than I'd imagined. Thank you."

She stuck the tip of her finger just inside me and held it there, in a tantalizing promise of what was to come. My cunt ached to close around it and suck it inside.

"Do you want me to fuck you?"

"Yes, ma'am. Please."

"I know you do. Not yet, though." She removed her finger. I groaned with frustration.

"All in good time," she laughed. "Can you take a little more for me first?"

I honestly didn't know if I could. My ass was throbbing. But something made me want to please her, this person I'd only fantasized about until today. "I'll try, ma'am."

"That's a good girl." She raised the paddle and let it fall with more force than her previous swats. I was unprepared for it, and I yelped.

"Just a few more. You're doing well for your first time." She continued at an even pace for a few moments more.

I had tears in my eyes when she was done, but I'd managed to take it all in stride without using my safe word. I was proud of myself. And I knew she would now reward me by letting me come. "Thank you, ma'am." I prepared myself for the touch of her hand on my cunt.

She caressed my ass with her palm, rubbing away the

sting. I wondered just how red my butt was after all that attention.

"What's next?" she teased.

"Whatever you wish, ma'am." I played my part.

"That's a nice touch," she laughed. "Come over to the bed."

She helped me climb on. It was hard to do without the use of my arms. I began to lie on my back but she stopped me.

"Assume the position," she commanded.

What position? The only position I knew about was head down, ass up. I thought of it as a punishment position, but surely we were finished. I realized I was taking too long to obey her.

"Ma'am? Permission to ask a question, please?"

"What is it?"

"What position are you referring to?"

"You know exactly what position I'm talking about, you insolent bitch!"

I began to panic. She sounded angry. I was confused, but I knew better than to test her patience. I lowered my head to the bed and raised my ass up in the air, not sure what to expect.

"It's time for your punishment," she reminded me. "You didn't think I would forget, did you?"

"No, ma'am," my voice was shaking. I didn't think I could possibly take any more whacks with that paddle.

She showed me I was wrong. She spanked me 10 more times, harder and faster than before. These slaps weren't designed for pleasure at all. Each one hurt more than the one before. I started to sob, but I didn't ask her to stop, though I was tempted to.

"That's all." She put the paddle aside and wiped the tears from my eyes. Then she kissed me hard. "I think you'll remember your manners from now on, don't you?"

"Yes, ma'am. Thank you, ma'am."

"Get up on your knees." She lifted me by my elbows until I was kneeling at the edge of the bed. "Now, spread your legs wide for me, and bend over."

It was an odd position to be in with my arms tied behind my back, and hard to maintain. I was exhausted from my beating and wanted to lie down, but I didn't dare.

Suddenly her hands were on my breasts again, fondling them, stroking my nipples. It was so stimulating I wanted to cry. She alternately rubbed and pinched my nipples. I didn't know what to expect from one moment to the next, but it all felt good. Her hand strayed down to my cunt, which was open and aching with emptiness. She entered me slowly with two fingers, and I leaned back to invite them in further.

She laughed. "No, no. We'll do this my way or not at all."

"Yes, ma'am. Sorry, ma'am." It was maddening. I was so hot by then I should have been a pile of ashes.

She continued to play with my breasts while she moved her fingers in and out of my soaking-wet pussy. Then she rubbed her thumb against my clit for a brief moment of glory. I saw stars and cried out. I was so close to coming. I wondered if I was allowed to come. What if she told me not to? I didn't think I'd be able to stop myself, and then I'd be punished again. I had no doubt about that.

"Requesting permission to come, please, ma'am."

"Oh, no. It's much too early. We have to play a little longer."

I whimpered and tried to concentrate on something else as her hands brought me closer to the edge. Gratefully, she stopped touching my clit. Now it was just her hand pumping my cunt. In and out she moved in a sensuous rhythm. All at once, she stopped. I heaved a sigh of relief. My stomach hurt from the awkward position. I hoped she'd allow me to rest for a while.

"I have another surprise for you," she taunted.

I didn't know if I could handle any more of her surprises. I was spent and frustrated from needing release. Suddenly I felt her hands on my hips and my cunt opening wider to receive a thick latex cock dripping with lube. She fucked me hard from behind, pulling my hips back to meet her thrusts. Then she let up for a moment, pulling out entirely. When she entered me again, I heard a buzzing and felt the vibrator deep inside me. She'd slipped an attachment onto her dildo, and it vibrated up against my clit with every plunge. Her hands returned to my breasts, squeezing my nipples in time with her movements. It was too much. I came with a loud groan and collapsed onto the mattress.

"Oh, you shouldn't have done that." She clucked her tongue.

My insides turned to ice as fear clutched at my chest. Did she really think I could take another beating? I was going to have to use my safe word if she came anywhere near me with that paddle. I tried to reason with her. "Please, ma'am. Show a little mercy. I don't think I can take any more."

"We'll find out just how much you can take," and with that she resumed my punishment. When I tried to evade her blows, she tied my ankles to the bed so I couldn't move. She lifted me to my knees and affixed a pair of clamps tightly around my nipples, making me cry out in anguish and surprise. She pushed me back down on the bed and continued the spanking. I closed my eyes and let the agony wash over me until I reached that plateau where pain becomes indecipherable from pleasure.

She took me there, one stroke at a time.

Before she left, she untied me and held me in her arms. She kissed me tenderly and we made love in a sweet, gentle fashion. Then she let herself out as I lay there, happily exhausted.

DrkAngl65... She had played out my fantasy to the letter. I only wish I'd gotten her real name. I've searched for her since then, but her screen name's been deleted. I wonder if I'll ever find her again, some night in a lonely chat room...

What do U like?

Sugar: My First Threesome

LUNA ALLISON

When I ran into Lisa that day on Princess Street, it was a complete surprise. I let go of Sarah's hand to embrace her.

Lisa and I had been traveling separately, and I'd wanted to see her while we were both in Kingston. She kissed me hello and then glanced at Sarah, her eyes a question. I didn't skip a beat. I knew she wanted to know who this woman was to me. I smiled warmly at Lisa and held her eyes a second too long. I told Lisa that the two of us were going dancing tonight and she should come. I could tell she was into it, the way her face curled up into that beautiful smile of hers. While she hugged me goodbye, nestling her face into my neck, I wondered if she could smell Sarah on me from last night. In that split second before we parted, I flashed back to the thigh-shaking salty hot sex Sarah and I had had in her guest bed about 12 hours before. Afterward, Sarah had run her cat-o'-nine-tails over me gently until I fell asleep. I thought about how much I love dirty sex that fades to gentleness. Then I snapped back into reality. Letting go of Lisa reluctantly, I took Sarah's hand again and told Lisa I would call her tonight before we went out. I smiled for the rest of the day.

That night, Sarah and I arrived at the bar. It was about 11:30 and Lisa wasn't there yet. I craned my neck to double-check the dance floor. I had a surprise for Lisa and I was impatient. Sarah and I ordered our drinks and looked around for a few minutes. I wasn't ready to go onto the dance floor yet, but my hips just wouldn't stay still. Not that I wanted them to, I was just intensely distracted by the heat in my cunt. I was feeling crazysexy.

I caught sight of Lisa and jumped off my stool.

"Hi," I said with a coy smile.

I took her hand and led her over to where Sarah and I were sitting. We were alone for a moment while Sarah was in the bathroom. I stripped off my shirt and showed Lisa her surprise. A skanky blue halter that shows off my beautiful belly all the way down to my hips where my pants hang loose. She drew her breath in sharply and took in the view. When she looked up again, she was grinning.

"Beautiful," she said, letting her hand graze my flesh.

We had first fooled around a week ago—after two months of sexual tension—and at the end of that first night, she had asked me to send her a picture of my belly. She loved its hard and soft parts, my belly ring, the shape of me, the soft blond treasure trail. I loved how she loved my belly and I wanted to give her something to think about when I wasn't there.

"Oooooh, I like you," she'd said. "I need a whole day to romp with you"

With a giddy smile, I told her that could be arranged. She asked if we could write dirty letters to each other. Oh, yes...she was the kind of woman I had been dreaming of.

Sarah came back from the bathroom. She crossed the entire room without taking her eyes off Lisa. They shared a curious smile. I should have seen this coming. You see, Lisa has had this obsession recently with sporty girls, and Sarah was wearing a backward baseball cap.

I started thinking about how sexy they'd look on each other, but bit my tongue. I had never been with more than one person at a time. I wouldn't know how to bring it up without feeling embarrassed. Besides, I didn't want to be disappointed later, so I tried to keep my fantasies in check.

"Let's go dance," I said. They nodded and came with me.

It took a while for the music to really heat up. Bad music is an epidemic at queer bars. It's a strange phenomenon. All that cheesy techno music and old disco.

After a while, Lisa danced over to me.

"When did you start dancing like this?" she asked over the loud music.

"It's true...my hips have found a life of their own," I said, laughing. I was getting wet, imagining the three of us piled into Sarah's bed, licking salty skin, kissing relentlessly, exploring one another's bodies.

We were dancing in a loose circle with shy eyes. But as the music got raunchier, we drew one another in closer. Dirty smiles. Curious hands. Then we were up against one another, our shyness vanishing. It looked like it wasn't going to be that awkward after all. I don't remember who kissed whom first, but soon it was hands on ass, tongue on tongue, lips on neck, heavy breathing in my ear. My hips tilted to catch all the friction, the rubbing, the up and down of our bodies getting hot together. It was just bright enough in the bar to feel watched.

I glanced past Sarah, looking at the rest of the bar. A few hungry-eyed women sipped their drinks slowly, transfixed. Some pretended not to look. Some registered shock at our openness. One woman licked her lips and drank it in. She knew what she wanted. I like that. I like to be watched. It gets me really hot. So I smiled into Sarah's shoulder, grinding harder, nastier. I wanted to give them all a good show.

I turned around to face Lisa. Our eyes connected, hot, bleeding with the heat. She breathed heavily, eyes fluttering. Her cunt was throbbing, I could tell. I grabbed her by the hair and yanked her head back the way I knew she liked. Her eyes rolled back slowly into her head. Her breath was thick with desire. Her back arched. She was at my mercy, her head leaning into my hand. She moaned and I gushed. I could feel the exhale of Sarah's grin in my hair as she leaned in to kiss my neck from behind. She bit down hard, sucked good and long, marking me all over with her teeth. Her hard love is some of the sweetest I've known. I felt her urgency, wanted her closer to me, no space in between. I wrapped my hands around her ass and yanked her into me. She gasped and melted—just the right blend of hard and soft. I looked into Lisa's eyes, could tell she was waiting for my touch as she rolled her hips to the music. I slid one hand down her back, traced a line over her hip and across her stomach. I toyed with the idea of plunging my hand down her pants and getting her off right there, but the music was good and I didn't want to get thrown out yet. I turned Lisa around so her back was to the rest of the bar, slid my hand between her thighs and held it there for her to rub against while we danced.

Prove you want it , I thought as I looked into Lisa's eyes.

Lisa leaned into me hard, like she wanted my whole hand, but she would have to wait. Sarah whispered that she was going to get a drink. My other hand was suddenly free and I knew exactly what I wanted.

"I need you against the wall right now," I said, staring Lisa down.

I pushed her toward the wall until her back hit. She

tensed at the smack of the wall, then relaxed. I grabbed her by her lovely boyish hips, knowing she was wearing those sexy boxer briefs underneath, just out of my reach. She tilted her hips, arched her back, wanting something to grind against. I slid my thigh slow slow slow into hers, gradually connecting with her cunt. We kissed long and hard up against that wall. I had her tight by the hair, riding my thigh. Soft moans escaped her lips as we writhed against each other. My hand was planted on her ass, her back pressed against the wall. I was feeling so sexy, and what we were doing was gloriously indecent. Oh, to be an urban slut!

I kissed Lisa deeply and released her hair. As I drew back from her, she caught my eye and nudged me back out onto the dance floor, bumping my pelvis with her hips, owning my space, staring me down.

"I need some air," she said, grinning slyly. Her hair was standing up in every direction and she absentmindedly reached up to smooth it as she slid past me and out the front door of the bar.

I reluctantly watched her slip out the door but decided to stay right there and dance. My hips started up again and who was I to tell them no? I was getting off on moving my body, on being watched for every nasty grind, swivel, thrust, knowing how hot I am on the dance floor. My hips aren't shy, though they used to pretend to be. They like to swing out and fill the dance floor. Let me tell you, no one complains.

Then *the* song came on. Perfect.

"Baby, can you handle this? I don't think you can handle this..." I sang to the rest of the bar, rolling my hips and slapping my ass in their general direction. The most teasing smile crept across my face.

I'm a stripper, I thought, *I'm the sexiest woman alive,*

dancing for me, dancing for you. I don't remember how long I danced like that...

Later, I danced across the floor for a sip of water and saw Sarah sitting near the speaker at the edge of the dance floor, still taking a break. I thought I would see if I could entice her into some nastier grinding with the swivel of my hips. She grinned up at me, liking the show, but she wasn't going to budge. We'd been dancing close, naughty and sweaty, for more than two hours, and she was done. I leaned in and kissed her, then sauntered over to Lisa. She sat on one of the stools near-by, and I sat next to her. Sarah came over and sat next to me.

"Do you need to go home tonight?" I asked Lisa with a cocky smile.

I knew she was staying at her mother's house while she was in Kingston.

"What are my other options?"

"Spend the night with me or spend the night with us..." I said.

"OK!" she said, beaming.

"Which one?" I asked, laughing because I was so in love with her eagerness.

"Both, Luna..." said Lisa.

I kissed her tenderly and turned to Sarah.

"Would you like to spend the night with us, because we're both into it..."

Sarah grinned and nodded, hopping off her stool.

On our way out, we passed an ex of Sarah's who'd been watching us for most of the night. Sarah suppressed a gig-gle. Such sweet, sweet revenge.

When we got back to Sarah's place, we were sweaty, wet, and smelling of smoke.

"Shower?" asked Sarah.

"Shower!" we both agreed, and all three of us tumbled into her tiny bathroom.

As we each passed under the spray, I thought about how I love the way women look in the shower. Watching the water trickle and flow down the curves of their bodies was making me wet from the inside out. Sarah pressed Lisa against the cold tiles in a kiss and I reached around Sarah and thrust my fingers inside Lisa's cunt. She bore down on my fingers and let out this guttural groan from the back of her throat. After letting her ride my hand for a few minutes, I took it back. I smelled her on my fingers and smiled. I slid the fingers of my other hand inside Sarah. She melted and shivered and swayed to the rhythm of my fingers fucking her. It was like being in an electrical storm standing between the two of them. I stood back to watch their bodies move in and out of the spray, cocked against each other, pent up after so many hours of anticipation. Kissing, groping, wanting, thrusting, getting rid of the useless space in between. I lay down in the tub, watching them from below, feeling the rise of my sweat and the fall of the misty spray on my skin. Sarah sucked hard on Lisa's lips and Lisa fucked her good.

I got onto my knees and worshiped Lisa's cunt while Sarah kissed her, touched her, bit her lovely full lips. I slid a few fingers inside Lisa and put one finger on her asshole, sure she would take it. She moaned, thrashing against my hand, and leaned back against the tiles with tilted hips. She threw her weight onto my hand and fucked me on her tiptoes. Her face got red and strained, she was close but wasn't going to get there. It was time to get out.

We wrapped ourselves in towels and chased one another down the hall to the guest room. I picked up Sarah's cat-o'-

nine-tails when I got there. Sarah bought it from friends of mine at the music festival where we met this summer.

Hmmm...I had never used one before. It felt good in my hand. I ran the soft rubber strands through my hand a few times and stared at those wet, naked women I loved on the bed in front of me. So much exposed flesh.

"Can I give you a little of this?" I asked Sarah.

She flicked her eyes over the tool I was holding.

"Yes..." she said, breathing heavily.

"What's your safe word?" I asked her.

"Mmm...sugar," she said, in between kissing Lisa. My face flushed. *That's fucking hot.*

"Lisa? Can I give you some?" I asked.

"Mmm...yes, a little."

"What's your word?" I asked

"Sugar. That's sexy, I'm gonna use that too from now on..."

I started dragging the ticklish strands across soft thighs, rounded asses, vulnerable breasts, and entwined legs. Slow. Sexy. Predatory. I wanted them to stop waiting for it, to lose themselves in their kissing again so I could draw gasps from my sudden blows. I drew it back and landed a blow on Sarah's ass. She jumped a little, exhaled deeply, then kissed Lisa hard, channeling the sensation. *Smack smack.* I started in on their bodies like a stern teacher, kneeling between them. *Smack smack smack. Smack. Smack.* Irregular, unpredictable, hard. I was in control and they knew it. I landed a hard blow on Sarah, then Lisa, leaving a red blotch on each of them.

"Sugar!" yelled Lisa.

"Sorry...I'll..." I started.

"No, my lip," said Lisa. Sarah was bearing down on it with her teeth.

We all laughed together at the irony, but I cut it short with the snap of my untrained wrist. *Smack smack smack smack. Smack. Smack smack. Smack smack smack.* Gasps, moans, startled bodies. God, this was too much. I was drunk with power.

When they had had enough, they were hungry for me. Their arms were reaching up to me and I lay down between them, wanting whatever they had to give.

"Can I fist you, Luna?" Sarah asked.

I nodded yes, so hot for her hand.

Lisa curled up next to me while Sarah snapped on a glove. Lisa was sucking on my nipples and whispering in my ear.

Sarah slid a few fingers into me easily, the glove slick with lube. She drew back her hand and thrust all four fingers in up to the knuckle. I whimpered. I wanted to give birth to her hand. I wanted her to stop keeping me waiting for that full beautiful feeling.

"Fuck me," I said weakly, almost a question.

She pressed into me and released me, slid her hand in and out of me, up to the hilt of her knuckles, pressed the hardest part of her hand into me. I pressed all the weight I could into her hand and met her eyes.

"Fuck me," I said louder.

She pushed into me so hard I thought I would come undone. I was making high-pitched noises like a puppy. I pressed against her with all of me. What I wouldn't do to take the world into my cunt. I wanted to expand and take in the whole room. I wanted a dick, a tongue, two hands, and a vibe at least.

"Fuck me!" I yelled, needing more and more, my desire expanding exponentially in each moment. It would never be enough.

"You are so beautiful," Lisa whispered into my ear.

She swept her hands across my nipples and made me shiver with love.

I strained and arched and wanted everything all at once. Close to tears, close to coming, close to true love. Sarah pulled out of me and buried her face in my cunt. She had made me come violently with her tongue the night before, and I'd screamed like a wounded animal. It felt so good that it hurt to see the end of the fuck. Her tongue set me off like fireworks.

Fuck fuck fuck fuck fuck fuck. This can't end. I was being bombarded with sweetness, and I felt like I would die if it stopped. Sarah slid her hand back inside me again, and the intensity was too much.

"Sugarsugarsugarsugar…" I said, slurring my words and trying to catch my breath.

Sarah withdrew her hand and studied me for a second before I sat up and crashed into her mouth, kissing her hard, my tongue fucking her. An intense thank you for her sweet sweet fucking.

Lisa started to kiss my neck from behind. The urgent, forward kisses of a woman who'd had enough of watching. I knew what I wanted, and I reached for a glove.

"Lisa?" I asked, turning to her as I snapped the glove onto my hand. She scrambled from sitting to lying down in record time. It made me feel like a gynecologist the way she scooched down in the bed—although I bet they never see that kind of eagerness. I slid in a finger or two. Added lube. Slid in part of my hand. Sarah watched in awe then moved to Lisa's breasts, kissing them tenderly, softly, sucking them in between her lips. Lisa squirmed at my touch. She had commented on my small hands earlier, and I didn't want to leave her unsatisfied. If there's one thing I've learned, it's that you can't keep a lady waiting.

I pushed my hand into her, back to a couple fingers, pushed my hand in again, drew it out until I was barely touching her, and thrust in again. I wanted her to feel the contrast, the pumping, the friction, the love. I was watching her cunt closely but wasn't looking in her eyes for her reaction.

"Sugaarr..." Lisa said. I looked up and there were tears running down her face. Concerned, I took back my hand and curled up on one side of her. Sarah was already on the other side.

We kissed Lisa and held her until she felt ready again, then we started over, slower this time. Sarah played with her clit while I worked her G spot. She was sopping wet and breathing heavy, soaking the bed with every buck of her hips. She arched her back, and in between loud moans and gasps she was directing us like a porn star, telling us exactly what she wanted.

"Oh, Jesus," she sighed. "Ooohhhhh...mmm...yeah... there! Oh, God God God God God..." Her body crumpled under the force of her desire.

Holy fuck. There is nothing like the feeling of the soft wet flesh of a woman's cunt.

Lisa bucked and strained and moaned and screamed, collapsing on the bed. After she got her breath back, she left the room for a bathroom break. She would be back soon, but in the meantime I was close to exhaustion and ready to come.

"Sarah, would you like to watch me get myself off?" I asked.

"Yes," she said with no hesitation.

On her knees beside me, Sarah watched my hand, my cunt, my face. I moved slowly, twirling the loose skin around my clit while my hips shifted from side to side, up and around. My breathing got more insistent, an in-and-out rhythm like a Portishead song. My hand moved fast, irregular, then rhythmic, faster, hotter. I needed lube, but I couldn't wait.

Then Lisa walked back in the room.

"Surprise..." I said to Lisa with what breath I had.

She collapsed on the bed and rolled onto her back.

"I'm not surprised you're playing with yourself," she replied, grinning with her eyes closed.

I laughed as stars exploded in my cunt, then collapsed from sheer exhaustion.

"That was beautiful, thank you," Sarah said.

I kissed her softly for a couple minutes. I love the feel of her tongue on mine, and I wanted to savor it. Afterward, Sarah went to her room and Lisa and I curled up on the guest bed and kissed. How pleased I was that the night didn't end at the club with awkward smiles and a kiss good night.

Rough Trade

JULIE MCKINLEY

My mother and father didn't love me moving to California. After all, it was so far from Connecticut, they feared they'd never see me. Yeah, right, more like never be able to keep tabs on me! They wanted to set me up in New York City. They offered me even more help (read: cash) if I agreed to a post-graduation stint in an East Village studio, but after four years of being on my own at Wesleyan, I was above such bribery. I packed up my Volvo station wagon and drove to San Francisco. I found an adorable two-bedroom apartment, right in the heart of the Mission District, with Jenna, another Wesleyan girl.

At first it was freaky to walk out the front door and step over some homeless guy sticking a needle between his crusty toes, but I guess I got used to it. I at least stopped calling the cops every time it happened. That's just part of life here, and really I just feel more urban and grown-up each time I'm confronted with the seedier parts of this city. Men try to sell me drugs every day as I walk home from the BART station. I can't decipher their code words—"shiva," "outfits"—but I know they're up to no good. Slightly less harmless men try to sell me bus transfers for a quarter, then there are the ones who aren't trying to sell me anything but just want to ask for a bit of money. Sometimes I help out and sometimes I don't. It's like living in a kaleidoscope, always someone rushing at me, wanting something. I feel a long way from Connecticut, and that's what I wanted.

I came to San Francisco because that's where my friends went after graduation and because I was accustomed to getting laid by girls on a regular basis while at Wesleyan and I heard that San Francisco is the only place where the girls are continuously getting it on. I mean, really, it's not like there's much else to do! Since the dot-coms went under there's very little work. Probably I'll have to move to New York at some point to get my career in publishing going, but right now I just want a vacation, a break. I want to play, and San Francisco is my playground. There are lots of cute girls who are in bands or have dance clubs or make art and stuff. Nobody is really doing anything serious, so there's lots of room for sex and partying.

It was Jenna's idea to have the house party. I said, "Jenna, who will we even invite? We hardly know anyone except some other Wesleyan girls, girls we already slept with in like sophomore year, girls we learned to fuck by fucking." I don't really need to revisit those awkward moments. I want to reinvent myself out here in California, with someone sophisticated who knows how to fuck. I go out to the dyke bars, but people don't look at one another. Everyone has their own little huddle of friends and they're not taking applications for new ones. Sometimes when I'm waiting for the bathroom the door swings open and not one but two girls walk out. They're smiling these smiles, pretend-embarrassed. They giggle and either make no eye contact or make defiant eye contact, like I'm going to yell at them for fucking in the toilet while I'm outside doing the jig because I have to pee so bad. I'm annoyed, yes, but mostly

I am curious, curious and jealous. How did they meet each other? How did everything between them speed up to the point where they took each other into such a scuzzy place, a bathroom, someplace where people, you know, pee and poo? How did they become so hungry for each other that they had no choice but to slip off into a place of such public filth?

At the lesbian bar I make all the eye contact I can without feeling desperate, but nobody really looks back, and certainly nobody invites me into the bathroom. Jenna is right, we have to have a party, and though it seems like a crazy idea, we have to invite a lot of strangers, a lot of people we have never met.

Jenna and I are unemployed. It's such a bad job market right now, and we both have a stash of graduation money, so we've decided to take it easy settling into our new lives. We've been so busy shopping for the apartment, decorating it with Christmas lights, sewing curtains, and shopping for furniture. Most of our things we picked up at thrift stores— it's just what you do here. It's awfully cute, though we laugh that our parents would die if they knew we were spending their money on used furniture! We buy our clothes used, too. It's more original looking. Sometimes, obviously, the designers copy that style and Jenna or I might pick up something at Nordstrom or wherever, but these lesbians in San Francisco are pretty hard-core. They can tell if it's not really secondhand.

Everyone in San Francisco dresses like they don't have any money, which I think is really cool. One, it's kind of like a competition where you've got to work really hard at coming up with a clever ensemble, and two, it's great to be in a place where people aren't obsessed with material things. I mean, for Jenna and me, it's a real relief, raised the way we were and everything. Jenna is even embarrassed of her car—a Land Rover, brand-new. I told her not to take it so far. You need to have a good car, at least. My parents would never let me drive one of these hunks of rotted steel I see in the Mission. It's fun to dress blue-collar, and I think it's good to not be so status-oriented with your clothes, but you don't want to really *be* that way. I mean, if I were in L.A., for example, I would be dressing totally different. I am clear on that. When in Rome, right?

So Jenna and I decide to put all our time into the party. She prints out these adorable invitations with a sexy old-fashioned pinup girl on the front. We go out to the lesbian bar and have a few hundred cosmos to get brave, then we hand our invitations to every cute girl we see. Really we only want to hand them to the butch girls, the cute ones with their short spiky hairdos and longer mohawks, with their little ties and sweaters and their workpants. Looking around the bar, sort of drunk, finally reaching out to these girls, I am struck by how much the place feels like a costume party. All the butch girls are dressed like nerds or auto mechanics, and one is even wearing a sailor suit. The girly girls are also dressed up, like they're in a hip-hop video, or like punk rock sluts. One has a cheerleading outfit on and one a nurse's uniform. We're intimidated to invite these girls but it would be so weird and bitchy not to, plus Jenna and I were both women's studies majors and should know better then to feel competitive with other women! At the end of the night we've invited everyone in the bar, even the bartenders. We've even had some conversations, though I can't remember much of them.

The next morning Jenna and I had such hangovers! We

walked down the street to the coffee place and sat there all afternoon giggling and getting worked up for our party, letting the caffeine perk us out of the day-after sluggishness.

Jenna decided to keep the upstairs part of our apartment, where our bedrooms are, off-limits to our guests. It's our first party, and since we don't really know anyone it seems weird to let them traipse through our private quarters. Plus, Jenna slyly adds, "What if we get lucky and want to bring someone upstairs?"

I was delirious with excitement, having not been laid since the night before graduation with this one girl who is totally a lesbian-until-graduation type. It was fun enough, but she wasn't my type. I liked these butch girls who dress like little truck drivers.

Jenna stocked our bar with bottles of Stoli and Bombay Sapphire, and I filled the fridge with six-packs of microbrews, all with different cute labels. We had both gone to Union Square the day before and bought new dresses, figuring this was one occasion where we could forget about dressing down. We both had that moment, around 8 o'clock, sitting in our cute apartment, the lights twinkling like a Mexican restaurant, the bar set up, the veggies and dips and salsas and chips and the big bowl of hummus and the toasted triangles of pita all arranged on the table that I had totally Martha Stewart–ed out on (carving vegetables into little flowers and then arranging real flowers in tiny bowls sitting in the middle of it), all dressed up in our new dresses, our MAC lipstick freshly applied. We were just so ready, and we had that moment, like: What if nobody comes? Nobody really knows us. Why would they?

Jenna started chain-smoking her American Spirits, and I fixed us some vodka tonics, plucking slivers of lime from the crystal candy dish and dropping them into the fizz. We sipped through straws so as not to mess up our perfectly reddened mouths. Then it was almost 9 and we were drunk. Thank God the doorbell rang, because you know how quickly the tears of self-pity can come when you're drunk! But the bell rang and we were instantly cheered. It was just some girls from Wesleyan, but it was enough to get things started. The bell rang again, and then again, and soon the room was filled with people, girls from the bar. It was such a bother to have to keep running to the door in our heels, so finally we just left the damn thing open.

By midnight the house was throbbing with people, all kinds of people, people I'd never seen. It was like an APB was put out into the city, far beyond the confines of the tiny lesbian bar where we'd distributed our invites. All sorts of people were pouring into our home. My eyes locked on a trio of boy-girls who had just wandered in and were looking my place up and down like they'd never been in an apartment before. They were looking around with strange expressions on their faces, then whispering to each other, then laughing. There was something sort of rude about them, but they were so totally cute I couldn't keep my eyes off them. They were dressed sort of like gas station attendants or something. Big baggy sweatshirts and dirty jeans, baseball hats with stains on the brim. They carried paper bags wrapped around wide bottles, and one said, "Oh, damn," when she spotted the bar. Then they capped their bottles and started drinking from our bottles. "The good shit," one commented. "Right on," the other said, and they laughed again, then I watched as they started grazing at the food table. One picked up one of my flowers and stuck it into her baseball hat, saying, "I like flowers." Who were these jokers?

Jenna, look, I nudged her, but she was busy talking to another strange new girl, whose costume, I thought, was not as authentic as that of the girls shoveling chips loaded with mango salsa into their greedy mouths. I wondered if they were showing off, but no, I figured their parents had cut them off and they were broke and honestly munching. Parents can really trip sometimes. Mine had sent me to a psychologist. Like that would work. But they think the wallet always will. I have some friends who are dealing with that—either cut off because they're gay, or because they have parents who want them to know what the "real world" is like or something. It's a drag, but I can't believe anyone's parents would keep it up forever! It's so mean. Anyway, the three girls with the best, most real-looking outfits had noticed me staring and had started staring back. "Hi," one said, but it wasn't a particularly friendly "Hi," it was more of an aggressive "Hi," like a dare.

I took the dare. "Hi," I said. "Hi, and welcome to our party."

"This is your house?" one of them asked. She was the cutest one, I thought, though they were all cute in their way. This one seemed a little bolder, and I was looking for bold. *It would take bold,* I thought, *to get me fucked in a bathroom.* Being fucked in a bathroom had become my number 1 fantasy. I looked the girl in the eye. Her eyes were dark, dark with faint circles underneath that made them look even darker. Her hair, beneath her baseball hat, had a curl to it. Her lips had a curl also. She was staring at me, hard.

"This is my house," I said proudly. "Me and Jenna." I pointed to the back of Jenna's blond head. "We're like sisters."

"You look like sisters," one commented.

"Oh," I said. "You just think all blondes look alike!"

Was I flirting? I was, brazenly, outrageously. Once I realized this, I flirted more. *Look at me,* I thought. *Look at me, flirting with strangers.* "So," I murmured to the cutie before me, "are you casing the joint, or what?"

She stared, then blinked. Then laughed a sudden, sputtering laugh, and looked at her friends with wide eyes. Some girls don't know how to be flirted with.

"Casing the joint?" she repeated.

"Yeah," I continued. "Did you and your friends come here to rob me? Drive my stuff away in your truck?" I paused, waiting for her to get into the role I was setting up for her. She came dressed like a little hoodlum; didn't she want to be treated like one?

"Yeah," her friend said slowly. "We're going to rob you blind. Hide your *jewels.*" Then she grabbed a mostly-full bottle of Stoli and slipped it under her jacket. Her clothes were so bulky you could barely tell she'd done it!

I giggled. "You're a magician," I told her. She was cute, too. I let my smile stay on her as she shifted the bottle around under her outfit.

"Hey, *I'm* a magician," the first one butted in. Were they fighting over me? I felt high on this attention.

"Oh, really?" I asked.

"Yeah, you want to be my assistant?"

"Sure," I gushed.

"Why don't you take me to your bedroom?" I was shocked at how bold she was. They must have been already drunk from their big bottles. The other two were laughing and shaking their heads. "You're too trashy for my bedroom," I teased. "*You,* I'll take to my bathroom." Clever on my behalf, I thought.

"Damn!" one of the others laughed. They shook their

heads and swallowed more food. I grabbed the original cutie by the scruffy cuff of her sweatshirt and tugged her up the stairs. She blinked at them. "You have an upstairs?" she asked.

"Yes," I told her, "and you are very lucky to be invited up here. It's strictly VIP."

"VIP," she repeated in a little grumble. We began to march up, the chaos of the party falling away beneath us. Alone with her, suddenly my witty bravado faded. "Um, where did you go to school?" I asked.

"I didn't go to school," she sort of snorted at me. Seriously, like not play-acting.

"Where are you from?" I tried again.

"I'm from here, and I didn't go to school."

I was taken back a bit.

"Oh, really?" I asked. "Are you, like, taking a year off?"

"Like, no," she answered, and I felt bitten by the mockery in her voice. "No, I'm not 'taking a year off.' I didn't go to school, I'm not going to go to school, and I don't really want to talk about school. Did you bring me up here to talk about school?"

We were in the upstairs bathroom now. It was sort of messy. Since we weren't allowing anyone to come upstairs, Jenna and I had focused on cleaning the downstairs and had neglected the upper half. I shook myself back into flirt mode, shut the door, and turned the lock.

"Well, I haven't been fucked since college," I said daringly. "And I've never been fucked in a bathroom."

"Really?" she said, looking me up and down like she couldn't believe me.

"Yeah," I continued. "And I never fucked a stranger before. And," I teased, "I never fucked rough trade before."

I loved the phrase "rough trade." It was so campy and silly and sexy at the same time. My gay boyfriends had always thrown it around.

The girl's eyebrows shot up. "Did you call me 'rough trade?'" She looked incredulous. She stared.

"Yeah, baby, I like rough trade," I played along. Who was I? Who talked like this? But I was getting to live out a little fantasy, right here in my own home, at my excellent first party, by a girl who was dressed like it was her fantasy, too, wearing the corresponding costume.

"Get over there." She pointed to the toilet. I started toward the bowl, but she lurched ahead, kicking the seat down with a jarring clatter. She even wore workboots. This girl had it down! She took me by my neck, her hand clasped strong around the back, and sort of pushed me forward onto the bowl. I was straddling it, my elbows leaning on the tank, and my back to this girl whose name I didn't even know. "Lift your dress," she said, and I obeyed. I was happy to be wearing my favorite new underwear, a little mesh thong held to my hips by the tiniest scrap of fabric. The girl wrapped her fists around them. Her nails were dirty, her fingers sort of grubby. Should I ask her to wash them first? Would that be rude? The girl wrapped her fists around them and then with a strong motion simply ripped them off my body. I gasped. It actually saddened me to see my new panties limp and broken in her hand, dangling there.

"Those were new," I blurted. "Those were new Donna Ka—"

"Shut up." The girl was smiling as she stuffed them into the pouch on her sweatshirt. She reached under me and pulled my ass higher into the air. She spit into her palm and started rubbing my pussy, rubbing spit all around it. We were being filthy. I promptly forgot about my new Donna Karan underwear. This girl knew how to do it, all of it. She had the act and she knew how to fuck. She rubbed me and rubbed me till I was just melting, and then she slapped my pussy, slapped it, then she went inside with her hand. I forgot about her dirty fingers. She fucked me like she'd been fucking girls like this all her life. She fucked me strong and sort of mean. She slapped my ass and pulled my hair. She wrapped my ponytail around her fist and yanked my head back, and when she kissed my lips her mouth was hard, she bit as she kissed, and I knew my mouth would show it when she was done. Everyone would know I'd been kissed like that, kissed like that and fucked on a toilet. She took her hand out and placed it, wet with me, flat on the front of my new dress. She spun me around, and with a little lift she had my ass, bare, on top of the cold tank of the toilet. I could feel the skin of my ass cheeks being gently exfoliated by the granules of cocaine left there from Jenna's private midparty rendezvous. She fucked me from the front now, so that I had to look her in the eyes, those dark eyes shadowed with the brim of her ball cap. She brought her face down and gave me another mean kiss, and I moaned.

"I love fucking rich bitches like you," she muttered into my ear, and I worked my hips harder around her hand. I had never expected to find someone so into "role-playing." If I'd known how much of a role-player I'd find, I would have pretended to be a waitress or something like those girls at the Lex, something sexier then just myself.

"Are you my assistant?" she asked, deep into my ear. Her voice was so low and hot I shivered.

"Yes," I croaked—my throat was dry from panting. She tugged free the ribbon from my ponytail, a thick black ribbon as long as my forearm. She pulled me up and dragged me to the shower, stretching my hands up to the shower curtain rod. She threaded the ribbon through my hands and around the bar, snaking it tight around my wrists. "Magician's assistants get tied up," she said absently, her eyes intent on her knots.

"Are you going to slice me in half?" I whispered. "Are you going to make me disappear?"

She laughed, moving away from me. She stood there in my bathroom, looking at me, and I felt, in her gaze, that I must look beautiful, that her eyes were making me that way, making me more and more beautiful the longer she lingered. "You are hot." She nodded slowly, and her voice sounded like she was conceding something. "You're too hot to make disappear." She smiled. She moved over to my sink and lifted a tangle of jewelry from the little ceramic dish. She took two necklaces—a white-gold and a yellow-gold one of Jenna's—then a white-gold bracelet, my toggle choker from Tiffany's that I wore almost every day (but not to dress up for parties), and my Elsa Peretti gold bean pendant, plus a couple of rings. The magician slid the jewelry into the pouch that held my torn underwear.

"Put them back," I said, pouting. "Put them back and come fuck me."

I felt relief when she came back and her hand slid inside me again. "I'll fuck you," she murmured. "But I'm keeping your shit. Isn't that what you want? Didn't you want me to rob you? I wouldn't have thought of it, you little brat. But isn't that your fantasy? You wanted to know if I was casing the joint, right? You wanted to get mugged, huh? By—what did you call me—rough trade? You think it's sexy to be broke, huh? To work for some asshole all day? I was wearin' my daddy's work jacket before it came *en vogue*..."—she smirked a crooked smile with those words—"...enough for your little friends to copy." Her fingers kept pace with her words as she growled low in my ear. "You wanted it, didn't you?" She didn't stop fucking me. It didn't stop feeling good, but it was real now, I could feel it in her voice, that she wasn't kidding and all along I thought she had been. I thought she was just some girl, maybe like someone I went to Wesleyan with, in her gas station attendant jacket and greasy baseball hat, but normal, like me. But she wasn't like us at all. I think she was poor. She didn't have money. She *was* laughing at my house.

"Oh," I breathed. It was partly from being fucked so well, and partly from surprise, and partly from revelation, from understanding.

"Oh," I said. "Oh." I looked into her eyes. "You hate me," I whispered. And she smiled. She kissed me again, less mean, and I kissed her back. She touched my face.

"I don't hate you."

Her thumb caught the corner of my mouth, and smeared a crimson trail of MAC across my cheek.

"I don't hate you at all," she said sincerely. "But I am going to take my share."

"No," I sighed, but I couldn't put up a fight. My pussy wouldn't let me. She withdrew her hand from inside me. Empty now, it still pulsed from all she'd done. "I'll be right back," she whispered, and wiped her hand off on the hem of my dress. She unlatched the door and left the bathroom, quietly closing it behind her. I hung there on the shower, my arms starting to cramp, wondering at everything—the vibrations in my body, my now-empty jewelry bowl. I felt indignant and embarrassed. *I've just been fucked by a criminal!* That's what I thought, but it seemed unbelievable. *My first criminal,* I thought strangely. My first everything. Robbery, bathroom fuck, anonymous fuck, fuck by someone who really knows how to fuck, dirty hands fuck, tied-up fuck, I was weak with it all and wondered if I should scream, shriek, for her, for anyone. I just slumped against the porcelain tiles. My arms trembled on the shower rail, the shower rail trembled, too, and I wondered if it would fall from the wall, and then what would I do?

It was Jenna who came for me, alone, thank God. The girl had said to her, "Your roommate needs you, upstairs in the bathroom." Then she grabbed her friends and left. They'd stolen a bunch of our shit—some bottles of alcohol disguised in those paper bags. The original bottles, empty of malt liquor, were stashed in the shower in the downstairs bathroom. They stole a couple CDs and Jenna's vintage poodle figurine from the kitchen and also a photo of me, framed, from the hallway. I didn't tell her about the jewelry; she was already so freaked out. "They were thieves!" she kept repeating. She was horrified. I was surprised I wasn't more pissed. She spilled some more coke onto the back of the toilet and snorted a line. "I can't believe that trash was in our house! I'm sick of everyone wearing this low-rent fashion," she fumed. "You don't know who the real thieves are, you know? How can you tell?"

The fingernails, I wanted to say. The boots, the smell, the way they look at you. The way they fuck, of course. Jenna looked at me, a sober cast to her face. "She was good, too, huh?"

I nodded. "They always are."

The Cheerleader

DC LEATHERMAN

Prologue

She was a tall, slender, bleached blond. A tall, slender, long-legged bleached blond. I met her that first night at La Madeleine's on the corner of St. Charles and Carrollton. She arrived in a cherry-red mother of a Lincoln—all buttered-biscuit shiny outside with smooth, snowy-white leather seats inside. Sitting on the café's patio that cool October night, I noticed the Lincoln first, then her. Her small, heart-shaped face peered out the windshield, looking very lost. As I stared, I suddenly had an overwhelming desire to go help her find her way to wherever it was she wanted to go. I think that's what got me—the lost look on her heart-shaped face.

She parked the cherry-red Lincoln a few feet from my table and opened the door. Slowly she slid off the snowy-white leather seats; I thought her legs would never stop coming. Finally she planted her feet on the parking lot pavement and stood, revealing that she was tall, really tall. My eyes followed as she glided past my table, through the door, and floated in. When the door shut behind her, I shook my head and admonished: *OK. Claire. Enough! Get back to the books.*

I'd been noticing women more and more, but I hadn't thought much about it. I'd been separated from my husband

71

for over two years, my three kids were grown, and it was the first time in all my 48 years that I had ever lived alone. I'd told myself, *Hey! You're in New Orleans. Enjoy!* And I had been.

I had my nose back in my cultural diversity textbook, diligently reading, when I heard this squeaky voice. "Is this seat taken?" I looked up and there she was. I just stared at her, mouth agape, then quickly recovered and said, "Oh, no... Sit down. Please, sit down." And she did.

We made nice-nice with introductions and small talk while she waited for the pimply-faced waiter to bring her order. Then, as we both sipped café au lait and she ate her Caesar salad and I ate the café's free bread slathered with the equally free butter and jam (I was on a student's budget), we began to talk. She talked, that is; I listened. She had this high-pitched voice that at first hurt my Southern ears. But soon the irritation left and I found myself watching her lips and thinking about her never-ending legs.

Like me, she was separated from her husband and was "divorcing the son-of-a-bitch as soon as possible!" We did Cliff's Notes life comparisons and laughed over stories we told of our soon-to-be exes. Well, *I* laughed, she cackled like a proud hen at egging time. Soon that didn't bother me either. I was enjoying our conversation and really enjoying looking at her. Especially her lips.

Things started to go sour as we finished our third cup of coffee. She paused between sips and pulled a cellophane-wrapped cardboard package from her purse. *She smokes! Damn! She smokes,* I thought. Hell, she more than smoked. I could tell by the ease with which she went through the smoker's ritual that she was a pro: Unwrap and crumble the cellophane; gingerly and evenly tear off the foil top; thump-thump-thump the package on some hard surface; pull one out; light up; suck down good and hard; purse lips; blow out forcefully. Like an ad for Virginia Slims, the woman smoked. And she had this "fuck you" style that blew me away. She'd tilt her head back, point her cute little nose and chin up to the sky, purse her cherry-red lips, and, with a force that seemed to part the clouds, blow bellowing streams of nicotine clouds up into the sky. Big, old yellow-tinted, nasty nicotine clouds that soiled the cool, clear October night sky. *Smoke from her lips. From pursed lips. From cherry-red pursed lips, smoky clouds she blows.*

I hated smoking. Never had smoked. Never wanted to. Never intended to. Hated being around smokers. *And she looks like Mount Saint Helen's,* I thought, *like a goddamn volcano!* As we sat, and I watched, I felt heat radiate off her, emanate from her like hot steam from an erupting volcano. Like steam from that hot lava shit you see on TV—from Hawaii or wherever. Steam from bubbling hot lava. *Hot lava, spilling up and over and down all sides of the volcano. Slowly oozing down all sides of the volcanic mound consuming all in its path.* Yeah, I decided, as we talked about our kids—that was what she was: a damned volcano. But I was the one who erupted.

After the smoking shit, I decided I couldn't afford to like her. She was rich, and she had a cherry-red Lincoln with the snowy-white leather seats, and she smoked like a volcano. She was definitely not my type. Oh, I was going to be nice and do all that Southern hospitality shit—like all us Southern women do. And that would be that, and I would go my way, and she would go hers. But I should have known. I should have known.

The last straw came: She told me she'd been a cheerleader in high school. She even bragged about it. And, *GAWD,* I hated those prissy cheerleader types in high school. No way could I like her. I figured she'd probably handled her pom-poms in the same fuck you style she now puffed her Slims. She'd probably tilted her head back, pointed her cute little nose and chin up to the sky, rah-rah-rah-ed, and did the jumping splits for the boys. Probably in the same sassy way she blew nicotine clouds from her pursed lips. From cherry-red pursed lips...

I decided to end the night after inhaling enough second-hand smoke to jump-start my way down the Road to Emphysema. I used the excuse that I had an exam the next morning (I did) and reminded her that she had told me she had lots of packing to do.

Strangely, though, I found myself offering, "Well, I know how hard moving is. If you need help, you can call me this weekend." She said thanks and promised to call me if she needed me. And we left it at that.

I walked her to her cherry-red Lincoln and watched as she slid behind the wheel and nestled her cute little ass on the snowy-white leather seat. "Nice meeting you, dearie." she said. *"Dearie!* I thought. *Boy, that's a new one...dearie.* She cackled and blew smoke in my face from her fifth in a row and said, "See you soon." She backed out and drove away, a trail of smoke streaming from the Lincoln's window. From cherry-red pursed lip bellowing smoke she blew....

I waved back as she drove off—relieved it was over—and went home to study. At least, that's what I told myself I was going to do. I really was going to study.

Foreplay

I got home, took off my sweatshirt, bra, and jeans, slipped into my tank top, and sat on my bed. I spread my books before me, put my pen behind my right ear, arranged blank paper by my side for note-taking. "STUDY!" I ordered myself. That usually worked. I had a 3.8 GPA and intended to keep it through graduation. "STUDY! Claire. STUDY!" Then it started: *I want to taste them. I want to taste them. I want to taste your cherry lips. Sassy chin, sassy chin. I want to run my fingertips round your sassy chin and down your snowy-white neck. Rich bitch. Rich and tall and long-legged.*

I vigorously shook my head. "Damn, Claire! Study, girl-friend!" But the thoughts pushed through in spite of my best efforts to keep them at bay. *I want to run my fingertips round your toes, up the inside of your long legs, up the curve of your calf, I want to run my fingertips.*

"Where the hell is this coming from?" I asked myself. No answer came. Sure, I'd left my bum of a husband, but not because...not because I wanted to screw women! I was in my first semester of grad school, I had to concentrate on getting through, getting that damned degree. I couldn't figure out what was happening. Whatever this was, though, it would not leave me alone; she wouldn't leave me alone.

I gave myself a good talking-to. "Yo! Claire. This is not on your schedule. Not on your agenda. Not on your calendar." I was already cluttered and overextended. Overextended and cluttered with all those esoteric, academic, smart-as-a-whip pursuits that consumed all my days and most of my nights. I had to graduate. I had to get a good job. I had to support myself. This had to stop. I lectured on and on, "There is no room for anything else. There is no room for anyone else." But she would not listen. She eased in, moved in. She honed in. That night, and every night there-after, she pushed and pulled and cajoled and persuaded and seduced me. After four nights of fighting her off, I let go. I finally and completely let go and let her in. With a rush and a flourish of my soul I let her in. With a 21-gun salute of my heart, I welcomed her. I decided, *Hell! I like what I'm thinking and I like the way I feel when I am thinking what I'm thinking. I like it a lot. A whole helluva lot.*

So, sitting there on my bed alone that fifth night, I did her. I had never done "it" with a woman. Had not even thought *seriously* about it before. But that night I did her from her head to her toes. I kissed and caressed and licked and finger-tipped whatever I could get my lips and my tongue and my fingertips onto and into, I did her. Like a pro, I did her.

I let my head go where it wanted to go and take my body along—and what a ride! And I came. And came...and came. I did not even have to touch myself. And it was so very, very good. Damn, it was good.

I had always hated those prissy cheerleader types, but now I wanted one. I wanted this prissy cheerleader. This tall, long-legged, bleached-blond cheerleader. This cheerleader with cherry-red lips and a fuck you style that blew me away. Guess I had always wanted me a long-legged, rah-rah, hot rich bitch—just never knew it. "And," I promised that night, "I am going to get one. I am going to get *this* one."

I had erupted. And I was totally and completely taken. Now every night at bedtime she'd be there, resting, sprawled, long-legged, and cocky on the chaise lounge of my being. She'd lie there like Scheherazade, seductive, with songs of a thousand and one nights on her lips, hot juices just waiting for me to suck and taste. A million times a day I would ask myself, *Where the hell did she come from, Claire? Where the hell did she come from? And where are you going?* I had not asked for her. *Oh, Claire,* I'd tell myself with resignation, *you know sometimes you get what you don't ask for*...I thought it had something to do with on-the-job training in humility and a forgotten admonition that *Yo, Mama! You ain't in control!* Because I really *was not* in control.

I didn't know where it had come from, but I knew for sure where the hell I wanted to go. She had ripped me open. She had exposed me. Exposed my hunger for her sweet taste, my thirst for her savory juices. She had exposed my undeniable ache for the touch and the feel of her. Exposed my insatiable desire for the smell of her. They were new feelings. Brand-new-to-me feelings. Deep groaning feelings. Desire-from-my-head-to-my-toes feelings. All-over-my-body feelings. Now, I wanted them. Now, I welcomed them.

Seduction

After that first night, and in spite of my intense, crazy-ass feelings and thoughts, I managed to be "just friends" with her—at least I thought so. For over a month I hid my feelings for her—until a casual Sunday afternoon in ice-blue November, just before Thanksgiving. We had been meeting for brunch at the Quarter Scene on the corner of St. Ann's and Burgundy every Sunday since that cool October night. I had helped her unpack and arrange her apartment and had even slept over—in the extra bedroom, of course. On Sundays we'd walk from our respective apartments: me from mine, down on St. Peter's near Rampart, and her from hers on Chartres, almost to Esplanade. I usually preceded her by a few minutes and secured our favorite table by the window facing Burgundy. There we watched the Sunday morning Parade of Queens, laughing as they cruised one another and pranced to and from the all-day/all-night bars.

We usually shared an order: I remember that morning was Eggs Benedict. We ate slowly, with coffee and conversation in between bites. Kids. Careers. Exes. Life-to-come. Too many *Oh-I-didn't-know-that* and *You-too?*s to count. That morning I wanted her so badly I ached. That morning her eyes were particularly green, her lips especially red, and her laugh more than inviting. I spoke sensible words to her—but my thoughts drifted to where they had gone every night since that first night. *May I touch your ear, please? May I trace the shape of it with my fingertips and caress its dangling lobe?*

"We are alone now," I remarked. We both nodded pensively in agreement. We were women alone...*God, you smell good. May I run my fingers through your oh-so-blond hair? Touch my hand again...please. I want to swim in your sea-green eyes...maybe drown there.*

We finished. I paid the bill. How could I not? "Claire, come on over to my place," she invited. Oh, yes! "It's quiet there. You can study and write. I'll just putter."

Was that a coy smile on her cherry-red lips?

"Sure..." I said—casually, I hoped.

My heart leapt. Beat ever so loudly. Thumping like thunder. I wondered if she could hear it. We walked briskly.

God, her legs are long—long and sexy.

It was windy. *Oh, my nose is cold. Is it running? Oh, my God, my nose is running!* Past Chicken Man all draped with feathers and bones we coursed. "Come on, girlies," he invited. "The bones tell all. Let me throw them for you and tell you about your tomorrows."

If he knew, would he tell her?

We ignored him.

Round past the Pub—lecherous gays flowed onto Bourbon and tittered like teens and groped one another without shame. *Could they tell?* Down past St. Louis Cathedral we wove through righteous straights as they streamed from its open doors into the Square. *Uptight, wound tight, tightasses...if they only knew what I was thinking!*

Down Chartres we went, passing within a half-block of Maurice's Croissant d'Or. The smell of his fresh, warm French pastries did not even tempt me. We saw ole weird Tom standing in front, talking to himself as usual, his nose pressed against the plate-glass window, licking the glass every other word or two. "You can smell him from here," she remarked. "He musta missed his weekly bath."

I laughed—casually, I hoped. *I want to hold your hand. I want to walk hand in hand with you all the way from St. Ann's to the Square and beyond. I want the world to know. Hell, I want you to know.* My teeth began to chatter, but not from the cold, and I thought: *Damn fool! You are a damn fool, Claire. What are you doing? What are you thinking? FOOL!*

Chartres—the last block before Esplanade. We were there. At her place. She fumbled with her keys. *Is she nervous, too?* She found the right one. Opened the wrought-iron gate. I brushed past her. *Too close?*

Carefully, she locked us in. *Does she always do that?* I made small talk as we walked through her patio. Her two vibrating cats wove their way through my ankles. Their feline motors were idling high in greeting. *Mine is too. I feel it from my head to my toes. Anticipation. They beg my warmth as I beg hers.* "They always like you..." she said.

"Uh-huh..." I replied. I didn't give a damn whether her pussies liked me or not.

She fumbled with her keys again. *She is nervous!* "Ah, here's the damned thing," she shrilled. In we both went—her pussies not far behind. *No one can see or hear us now. No one.*

"Make yourself comfy, dearie." *Does she have to always call me dearie?* I tossed my coat on her red leather couch and sank into her overstuffed chair right next to the 8-foot window with the view of her patio. I propped my feet up on her glass-top coffee table, pulled my notebook from my backpack, and spread it across my lap. I stuck my pen behind my right ear and pretended to be studious. *Dear God, how am I going to get through this? I only want to touch her. I only want her to touch me. How?*

Out of the corner of my eye I watched her reflection in the gilded mirror hanging opposite her kitchen on the living-room wall. *She is tall. She is slender. She is blond.* She puttered in her kitchen, doing this and that. *Come in here and putter me! Now!* I shouted in my head. *Come in here, woman! Woman...please...*

She did.

She turned and smiled and walked toward me. *Had she read my thoughts?* She tossed the yellow towel on the blue marble countertop and came swaggering toward me. *Is that a gleam in her eye? Is that a gleam I see? Oh, she's coming. Damn! She's coming.*

She stood behind me. Her Estée Lauder hung in the air. My nostrils flared. She leaned and read over my shoulder—or pretended to. Her breath caressed the nape of my neck. Goose bumps began. She rested her warm hands on my shoulders. She leaned further into my back. *I feel her. Oh, yes, I feel her.* Her fingertips lightly kneaded my flesh. I closed my eyes. *Deeper, please. Deeper. May I take your hands into mine? May I place them over my breasts? Feel the hardness there. Feel what you have done to me? May I have your fingertips, please? Just for a moment...to place in my mouth. To suck, one by one. Your fingertips, please.*

She reached down, round my front. Her hair brushed my cheek. *Ahhh...goose-bumping!* Her right arm went round my neck. She braced herself and plopped her ass down on the left arm of her overstuffed chair. Her warm belly caved into my elbow. *I want to bury my face in your belly and below...*

Giggling, she slid off the arm and scrunched her fanny onto my left thigh. *HER ASS IS SITTING ON MY LEG! Her ass is sitting on my leg! Oh, God!* She slid her legs between mine, prying them apart with her bony knees. My knees went weak and I trembled. She laughed and grabbed the pen from behind my right ear. She teased me: "Now, let me see all your silly words," and her breath rushed into my face, smelling of ripe pears.

She held my notebook in front of her and stuck my pen between her pouting lips. *I want my tongue to be there. There, between your pouting lips. Go ahead and read my silly words. My rhymes of you.*

I looked at her heart-shaped face. She avoided my eyes. *May I take your face into my hands, please? May I pull your face to mine? And kiss your lips. Hard. Feel my lips tingle? Taste my hungry tongue? You need only one hand. May I borrow the other, please? May I take your hand and slip it between my trembling legs? Legs you splayed. Can I guide your hand to my warm wetness—waiting there for you?*

She read—or pretended to. She smirked, took the pen from her mouth, and drew silly smiley faces all over my poems. She laughed at me and tossed my words on her table. As she slid the pen back behind my right ear she looked squarely into my face, into my eyes for only a moment, one brief moment. *OH! YES! Yes, I see it there. I know you know. Your eyes say so. Don't go. Please don't go!* She slid off my leg, stood, and traipsed back into her silly kitchen, cackling. She picked up her silly yellow towel from her silly blue marble countertop and, still cackling, started wiping dry her silly dishes. She wiped her silly dishes dry.

I slumped down into the overstuffed chair. I was exhausted. I was spent. I was spent and wet. But I still had the night. I still had the night and the hope that in the darkness of this cold November night she would beg my warmth.

Climax

Mary Griffin was in rare form that night at the Mint. I finally had been able to study and needed a break. We both agreed we needed a Mary fix and walked the few blocks to the nightclub on Decatur and Esplanade. My friend Ashad was there and bought us drink after drink. We took turns dancing with him, his friends, with each other. We drank and we danced. We stayed until Mary's last song, then stumbled, holding each other up, the few blocks back to her apartment. Giggling, we crawled up the stairs. As we reached the top, before I could turn right to go to the guest room, she grabbed my hand. "Oooooh…dearie… It's too cold to sleep alone tonight… Come sleep with me, Claire."

I paused and my heart sank and met the butterflies in my stomach. "Uh, sure…sure." I followed her into her bedroom. She wasted no time pulling off everything as I stood in the middle of her bedroom, staring. Had she done this before? Then, there she was, as I had always wanted her: Tall and long-legged and naked, buck-ass naked with her dark blond bush making a "V" where it met her flat belly and her long legs.

"Now, dearie," she laughed, walking toward me. "I'll take off your little ol' shoes." And she pushed me back onto her bed and did just that. Then she leaned over me, dangled her tits in my face, and proceeded to unbutton my blouse and unzip my jeans with a deftness that belied her inebriation. She grabbed the hems of my jeans and pulled them off. Her eyes widened and she smiled when she saw there was no underwear to complicate her life. She cackled, dropped the jeans to the floor, and collapsed on the bed beside me.

"Take the rest of your damn clothes off yourself, dearie! And you'd better work fast, before I pass out... You silly, silly, woman... I figured I'd better do something. You never would!"

And so, I did. I stood, quickly slipped out of my blouse and bra, and lay on the bed next to her. I shuddered and my knees went weak as I felt her warm skin against mine.

In spite of all my practicing, I did not know where to start, and she voiced no preference. I was on my own. So I began doing what I had rehearsed in my head almost every night since that first week. I stretched out next to her, propped my head in my left hand, and with the fingertips of my right hand began stroking her blond hair, then the brow that framed her sea-green eyes, her flushed cheeks, her cherry-red lips, her pointed chin, her snowy white neck. My fingertips traced a circle around her tits, then, in my thumb and forefinger, I held each tip and gently rubbed them till they formed tiny pebbles and she moaned...and her back arched... Down her belly, past her navel, my fingertips tripped. At her bush they paused and curled slowly through, then continued down to the top of her thighs. Down to the bend of her knee, to her toes, I traced. Then I sent my fingers up again, along the inside of her calf, of her thigh. All the way up her long legs, my fingertips crawled...to her V...to her mound...to her volcanic mound. Into her hot lava, I dipped my fingertips. In and out, stroking the sides of her volcanic mound. In and out, dipping and stroking, dipping and stroking, my fingers...just like I had all the nights before in my mind...

I want your hot lava on my fingertips, on my tongue, on my lips. I want your hot lava to flow down my chin. I want your chin to tilt back. I want your head to tilt back and I want your sassy chin to tilt up to the sky. I want your lips to purse, your cherry-red lips to purse and puff and blow. No Virginia Slims. No plumes of smoke. I want to hear deep moans from your cherry-red lips, and high-pitched sighs...and a long Ahhhhhhhh...I want you to "RAH! RAH!" Rich Bitch. I want you to "RAH! RAH!" and shake your pom-poms and do the splits. Yes! I want you to do the splits...but not for the boys...for me...the splits for me.

I knew it was time... Before I started to go down, I lifted my face to hers and paused to look into her sea-green eyes. Her cherry-red lips parted but said nothing; her eyes gave permission. Never had I actually done this with or to a woman—nor had a woman ever done this with or to me, but doing it that night made me feel like a 5-year-old learning to swim. I felt wild and untamed and loose and free with Wondrous Untold Possibilities. Wild and Untamed and Free and excited to be alive...and excited that I could feel the way I felt.

Gently, I splayed her long legs and heard her sigh a sigh. Slowly, I stretched myself between her thighs. Gingerly, I parted her lips with my fingertips. I paused to inhale her scent and my nostrils flared. Then I entered her and my tongue found warm, salty juices. Unhesitatingly, I began to lick and suck. Slowly at first, then with a frenzy. A frenzy for her. For *woman*. For *women* I had never had. That I would now and forever want—forever need.

I felt her hot juices flow up and over and down all the sides of her, flow down and through all her cracks and crevices and nooks and crannies. I felt her hot lava flow down and I hungrily ate her. My tongue dipped and stroked, dipped and stroked. Soon my tongue found her throbbing hardness and my lips secured a purchase there and did not let go, did not stop. I did not let go, I did not stop until I heard her moan, until I felt her throb and pulsate, until I felt her buck, felt her hips rise against my mouth. Not until she pushed my face away and pulled it up to hers did I stop. As our lips met, she sniffed her scent on my mouth and lips and tongue. She sucked her juices from my lips, from my tongue, and came again and again...

I forgot books and pen and paper and grad school and GPAs and exams and all else. And, as we lay entwined, spent, sharing warmth that cold November night, I finally knew. At last, I knew, I was where I was meant to be, where I had always wanted to be. I was home.

And, I thought as I drifted off to sleep: *I got me my cheerleader.*

Epilogue

I was at her beck and call for another month or so. I screwed her whenever she wanted to be screwed. She had me; I truly could not help myself. Soon, though, I realized I was not part of her future plans. So, gradually and painfully,

I weaned myself off her tits and went on with my life.

I kept up with her through the French Quarter rumor mill. I knew that after me she had gone on to screw—and be screwed by—numerous other women. It hurt, but as time passed, it hurt less and less. Then, one gorgeous spring evening, my girlfriend and I decided to go to for a late-evening meal at my favorite café, Louisiana Pizza Kitchen, right across from the French Market. As we strolled hand in hand through the little café on our way to the outside tables, I saw her. She was sitting at a corner table with a decent-enough-looking, middle-aged male in expensive slacks and a sports coat. When she saw me, fear came over her heart-shaped face. I can't say I wasn't sorely tempted to go up to her man friend, tell him I knew his date in the biblical sense, and ask if she screwed him any better than she had screwed me. But, being a polite Southern woman, I simply smiled, said, "Hi, how are you?" and introduced my girlfriend. We made nice-nice for a few minutes, then went on our way, with me relieved that I felt absolutely nothing save amusement. I found out about three months later that she had married that man, that he was a doctor, that he had been in the Big Easy for a medical convention, that they had met and fell in love "instantly," that he had whisked her away to Chicago where they were to happily-ever-after live. Two and a half years later, the rumor mill ground out their divorce.

I have no idea where she is now and don't care. But I have to thank her. Really, I do. I found myself that night because of her.

Guilty Cleansing

J.J. RYAN

Aye, aye, aye, that ass of hers! Narrow from the waist, curving full and tight along the sides, and where the butt crosses the thighs there is no line to be seen. It just flows gracefully around and back up to her long waist. Her breasts are so full and beautifully shaped. They're large, firm pears, so perfect that the first time her eyes feasted on them, Gwen swore they had to be bought and paid for. For the record, they're as natural as the sun. Everything about Jamie was and is sensationally sexy. Especially her self-confidence and her laugh. And even though it could have been a problem, Gwen discovered that Jamie's guilt over the pain she had caused her ex-lover was also about to be another excuse for unimaginable lust and erotica. That overwhelming guilt gave her an opportunity to live out her fantasy as a way of life!

"What's wrong, baby?" Gwen asked, trying to sound more compassionate than disappointed. This was sadly becoming the norm. They'd been going full steam for about an hour this time when Jamie started to get weird again. Fading off into the distance…all body but no soul.

"Nothing," her lips replied, but her sad eyes spoke volumes. "I'm sorry," she relented as her little-girl eyes glanced downward, all apologetic and ashamed.

"I can't help you, honey, if you don't tell me." Gwen's fear was that the problem would be that Jamie wasn't getting over her last lover as well as she had wanted to believe. She turned onto her side and, facing Gwen, she pulled the sheet up over her shoulder. Gwen stared into her face and brushed the hair from her glistening brown eyes. Though Jamie's eyes glared in Gwen's direction, she looked through her rather than at her. The first time Gwen saw Jamie's eyes was on the dance floor at a girl's bar. The lights made her eyes look transparent. She thought if she looked long and deeply enough, she could see right into Jamie's mind.

If you asked Jamie, she'd say Gwen did read her mind, because though Gwen made the first move, Jamie wanted to spend time with her as well.

Gwen wished she could read her thoughts on this night especially. She wanted to help her. She would do anything she could to ease her pain, but she had difficulty reaching her when she was like this. Jamie is totally uninhibited sexually, always ready for something and anything. She is hot. Steamy hot, sexy, fun. She's able to laugh at herself, and Gwen finds that a real turn-on. They were always fucking, playing, kissing. They simply could not get enough of each other. Gwen thought she didn't even know what a simple kiss was anymore, because from the minute she braved kissing Jamie, she found herself drinking her in. She sucked and swallowed and lavished in every taste Jamie had to offer. She still does.

Jamie came out of her gaze.

"I don't know," she began. "I love you, I love making love to you, I love everything about you, and I don't know why sometimes I just feel almost sad or like I'm doing something I shouldn't be doing." Tears welled in her eyes. "You don't deserve this." She covered her face with her hands.

"What do you mean, sad? About us? About what? Tell me. Say it anyway you can, and we'll just break it down from there." Gwen was digging, not sure she really wanted to find the answers. Jamie closed her eyes letting Gwen wipe the tears underneath her lashes. She remained that way for a second or two, then let out a sigh. Gwen's heart skipped a beat. Here it comes, she thought to herself. All the things Jamie could possibly say raced through Gwen's mind. Things like, we jumped into this too fast. I still love Laurie. Let's stay friends. Too fast, too slow, too much, not enough...

"I mean that I feel so guilty," she said, interrupting Gwen's train of panicked thoughts.

"You feel guilty?" Gwen pounced, slightly relieved. "How do you mean? About Laurie?"

"I guess." She paused. "I feel like it's my fault that she moved back to California. Like she had to get away from me. I know she's hurting so badly, and I can't stand it."

Now it was Gwen's turn for a sigh. She knew Laurie, too. She knew Laurie even before she knew Jamie. She met Jamie through Laurie, and she still cared about her friend. When Gwen met Laurie, she was going through this nasty breakup with a woman named Jamie, whom she felt was cheating on her. Gwen listened to three months worth of this long, sad story, and her heart went out to Laurie. Laurie distinctly referred to the time period as "going through her breakup." Why it is that lesbians "go through" a breakup rather than just break the hell up, will anyone ever know? It's always this long, involved, overdone, drawn-out piece of hell, or it just isn't a lesbian breakup.

Time and time again, we step into a whirlwind romance, ride the surf high and low, and most of the time the wipe-out lasts longer than the damn ride.

"Listen, Laurie wasn't innocent. She's a big girl, and we both know why you looked for something else. I'm not saying I condone it, Jamie, but I understand it. Give yourself a break, already."

"I know," she said, and started to sob.

It's a bitch, how that completely melts Gwen's heart. Jamie's face when she cries is almost more of a turn-on for Gwen than her laughter is. Gwen aches when Jamie hurts. Although her heart hurts for Jamie's pain, she'd be the first to admit that between her thighs she's throbbing and wet 10 seconds after the first tear falls down her cheeks. It turns her on like nobody's business.

"Come here, baby girl," Gwen beckoned. Jamie slid over and tucked her head into her lover's open arm. As she traced Jamie's shoulder lightly, a tear tickled her skin when it slipped down her breast to the sheet beneath them. She squiggled, ever the princess and the pea, and Jamie shifted to a sitting position. Gwen casually wiped the wet trail and, taking Jamie's hand, brought her fingers up to her open mouth. She held them there, kissing each one and nibbling each tip. "Listen to me a second, OK? You can't ever go to her and tell her that her suspicions were right. You have too many mutual friends, and we both know that it'll be all over the place right after you tell her. That's not what you want.

"What you need to do is just forgive yourself your share of the damage and move on. Let her deal with figuring out that she wasn't totally blameless, and she'll move on, too." And almost without taking a breath she added, "Have you ever heard of a cleansing spanking?"

Loud silence. Long silence. Then...

"A what?" she inquired with eyebrows scrunched.

"A spanking for the sake of cleansing your guilt," Gwen responded. "Name to yourself all the things you feel totally responsible for, and then release it through a spanking." Jamie's interest was peaked. Gwen had read about this. It did make sense. And yes, a bit shamefully, it made Gwen horny. "Look, do you trust me? Do you trust that I would never hurt you? That I love you?"

"Yes," Jamie whispered, looking like a little girl. Butterflies floated in Gwen's stomach. Jamie lowered her eyes to the bed.

"Listen, you think about it a little. If it's something you think you're interested in trying, you let me know, OK? Just come to me whenever you're ready. I love you, Jamie. You don't have to think of it as me giving you a spanking. Think of it in whatever way makes you feel right. It's you that's punishing yourself every day now, anyway. So in a sense, it's you administering the punishment, only once and for all. And anyway, when a person submits to a spanking, for whatever reason, they are the one who is actually in control. You give me permission to open you up to forgiving yourself."

Gwen truly had no clue where these words or rationale came from, but they sounded right and she spoke with confidence. Jamie nodded and lay down on her back. Leaning over, Gwen gave her a kiss on her forehead. They spooned, and Jamie quickly fell asleep, while Gwen stewed for hours. All she could think about was how she would pull this off, making sure to accomplish exactly what she promised but still deliver in the passion department. She decided right before finally drifting off that there was no reason they

couldn't combine a little business and a little erotica, to satisfy both need and desire.

The next morning Gwen awoke to the sounds of Jamie's
shower. She heard the shampoo bottle go down on the shelf
and that told her there was at least another 10 minutes
before she'd be turning off the water. She decided to wait
until she knew Jamie had rinsed her thick mane before step-
ping into the shower with their favorite body oil.

Gwen padded barefoot into the second bathroom,
brushed her teeth, and pulled her hair into a ponytail.
Grabbing the oil bottle and an extra towel, she went into
their bathroom and flung the towel over the cabinet.
Through the obscure glass door, she could see Jamie standing under the showerhead facing the wall. Jamie leaned forward and placed her palms on the wall in front of her, allowing the water to bead over her arched back. Gwen stepped
in behind her, letting just enough cool air flow in so Jamie
would realize she wasn't alone. Jamie settled her back into
Gwen's body, signaling a request for a breast massage. She
rested her head onto Gwen's shoulder and melted right in.

"Did you give any more thought to what we talked
about last night?" she asked, cupping Jamie's breast.

Jamie stilled for a second. Was that a slight tremble they
both felt run through her body?

Taking advantage of the moment, Gwen slid her open
hand over Jamie's belly and down to the silky place between
her legs. Gently, she pulled the tiny hairs a few at a time,
making Jamie buck lightly and squirm a bit. "Well, did you?"

Closing her eyes, she replied, "Yes."

Still pulling and twisting the tiny hairs on Jamie's
mound, Gwen continued to press her.

"So, what do you think? Does it make sense to you?"

"I've never been spanked before. Well, not really." This was spoken with more breath than voice.

"Well, it isn't a play spanking anyway, you know. I know you and Laurie used to fool around a little, but if this is gonna work then you have to understand what it's about. You'll submit to a true spanking and give over any guilt you still have. It isn't a game, Jamie." Gwen placed her palm flat against Jamie's upper back, gently forcing her forward slightly. With her right hand still cupping Jamie's treasure, she coaxed her into a deep forward bend, causing Jamie to throw her hands on the wall in front of her. She steadied herself as Gwen suddenly gave Jamie's rump a firm slap and determinedly inserted her fingers inside her inviting pussy, pumping her with abandon till Jamie was forced to rest her cheek against the cold, wet shower wall. Gwen pulled out and turned her around. Pressing her mouth against Jamie's, Gwen kissed her wildly, hoping they could rekindle some of the passion of last night...

Jamie stood on the carpet, her legs spread slightly, giving her balance as she towel-dried her hair. Gwen loved the way the baby oil made Jamie's tan glisten. She was so captivated by this girl. She sat Indian-style on the bed, waiting for Jamie to notice her. So what would she say this time? How would she bring up the subject again, this time getting a straight answer, a commitment?

Absorbed in her thoughts, she almost missed that Jamie was finished drying her hair and getting ready to dress.

"Baby girl, come here a minute."

"What, honey? I need to get dressed."

"I wanted you to know that I'm serious about what I

said, but if you want to drop it that's fine, too. It's up to you, and I won't bring it up again. OK?"

Gwen had obviously decided to play the reverse psychology card. She had felt Jamie stiffen and quiver in the shower when she mentioned it. She could tell that even if a spanking scared her a little, it also intrigued her. Gwen wanted a few things out of this, but Jamie would gain from it as well. She wanted Jamie to feel free again to enjoy herself without guilt was as much out of concern for their sex life as it was out of concern for Jamie. She also loved the idea of dabbling in a little D/S, and this could be a way to introduce it to her lover. Jamie seemed open to anything they could enjoy together, but Gwen always felt ambivalent about bringing it up.

"Actually, no, I was thinking that it would help." A long pause followed, and then, "If you want to, we can figure it out, OK?"

Gwen was shocked and excited. "Sure, angel," she replied, and trying not to look too eager, she added, "if you're sure."

That evening after dinner Gwen suggested they have drinks by the pool. Jamie responded by biting the lower lip of her smile and her eyes grew wide.

"Cool, wanna take a dip? I'll get the towels."

"Uh, yeah, sounds good." Jamie took the plates into the kitchen and started musing over the possibility that tonight could be the night they would carry out their cleansing ritual. Somehow naming it endorsed it for her. Truth be told, she wasn't convinced that it would do anything to ease her guilt over what she'd caused Laurie, but by pretending she did believe it, this would give them license to take the chance. So it was that a little submission turned on our innocent little Jamie as well. Who'd have known?

When she got out back, Gwen was already sitting on the steps of the pool.

"Oh, you're quick," Jamie laughed, spying the tray with the components of tequila shots and a cosmopolitan—and upon closer inspection she noticed that Gwen was frolicking waist-high in the pool, sans a bathing suit. Gwen saw her surprise and simply smirked. "Come in," she said, "it's almost warm."

Jamie complied: Pulling her T-shirt over her head and kicking off her sandals, she dove in. Gwen caught her under the water and stripped her of her panties. They volleyed the beach ball, swam, made out, and played. Gwen made her way to the edge of the pool and pulled herself up to rest on her elbows.

"Where are you going?"

"Getting something. Come here."

Jamie waded over and snuggled up behind her. Gwen took a small piece of lime and slowly dribbled some juice over Jamie's breast. She circled the nipple with the wedge. Jamie leaned back on the stone ledge. "Mmm, add salt and nibble."

That's exactly what Gwen did. She licked and she sucked…

…Later that night as they lay in bed, Jamie turned away from Gwen. She inched her way backward to spoon.

"Now that's different," Gwen giggled. "What's up?"

In her best naughty girl voice Jamie replied, "I want you to give me my spanking."

Gwen did all she could do to conceal her enthusiasm. She held Jamie tighter from behind and eased her head into the crook of her neck, her lips close to Jamie's ear.

"It would be my pleasure," was her cool and composed response. It took all the willpower she could rally, but she thought it best to end the conversation right there, knowing full well that showing any signs of fervor may have sent Jamie running the other way. She had to make Jamie believe that this was nothing but a therapeutic endeavor to rid her of the guilt that was taking away from her happiness in a new relationship. What a pity it would be if Jamie were to change her mind. God forbid, Gwen thought to herself. She smiled and tried to get some sleep. Jamie admitted to herself that she was more than a little disappointed at Gwen's lackadaisical attitude. She reached down between her legs.

Still wet and swollen, she contemplated waking Gwen for another go-around, but feeling a little hurt at her inattentiveness, she decided to use the spare room to spend her lust this time. She was feeling naughty and acting spoiled, but she tiptoed across the carpet and into the small bedroom. She left the door slightly ajar because she didn't like the dark. The dim hallway light was just enough. Jamie crawled onto the daybed and quickly busied herself. She was surprised at how on fire she was. She probed and caressed and closed her eyes and dissolved into herself.

At the very second that she arched her tense back, causing her breasts to point to the ceiling, just as she grabbed the bar on the headboard with her only free hand, she felt the breeze from the doorway and could sense the light. She opened her eyes to see Gwen at the end of the bed with her head cocked and her eyebrows raised. She could tell she wasn't angry, but the look was like the cat that caught the mouse, all the same.

"Having a good time, yes?" she posed to Jamie with sarcasm and an air of authority.

"I didn't want to wake you up," she managed to sputter, adding, "Join me?"

"Not this time, kitten, and waking me wouldn't have been a crime, you know. Neither is this, for that matter, but I can't say that I don't feel a little left out."

A little embarrassed at being caught in the act, and especially at that very moment, Jamie grabbed the throw blanket and haphazardly covered herself as she sat up. Nervously, she brushed the hair out of her eyes and then fiddled with it till the bangs were back in front of her eyes again. Gwen knew the gesture indicated she was feeling nervous and submissive. She realized what a perfect position she was in now. Complete control. This was her moment to shine. And shine she would. Her whole body pulsated.

"Tell ya what, little girl. You have no reason to feel ashamed or guilty, but if you do, well, then, you do." She walked over to Jamie slowly. Standing over her, she lifted Jamie's chin up with her index finger. Sternly, she ordered, "Get your pretty body up, and go to the bedroom. It seems like you have an unhealthy view of the pleasures of sex, with me and with self-gratification." Jamie looked into Gwen's face. One eyebrow cocked higher than the other usually meant Gwen was upset. She could feel her wetness return. Her response to the way Gwen was handling this just floored her. She was so turned-on. Jamie wanted to be disciplined for what she hoped Gwen would consider an indiscretion. She had never felt this way before. Gwen, on the other hand, was right on Jamie's trail. Gwen would play this deal of a lifetime with all the care and charm she had ever imagined. "I'm serious! You definitely have issues, and I intend to take care of every one of them, no matter how long it takes."

Jamie was practically about to orgasm; she could feel it and feared Gwen would realize it, too.

"Go into the bedroom, I'll straighten up in here and be right in. OK?"

"OK," was the only reply Jamie could spit out. Jamie stood up, keeping the blanket close to her, but she felt it torn abruptly from her hands.

"Go out the way you came in. I deserve that much at least, yes?"

"Yes," she managed, and walked out without so much as looking back even once.

Gwen waited about 10 minutes before returning to the bedroom. She was horny and wet and wanted to calm down first because she wanted to show indifference. She knew this would make Jamie wild. She wanted her hot and out of control like back in the beginning, and she knew this would do it. Jamie, on the other hand, was fuming. She was deciding between feigning indignation and conceding to submitting for therapeutic purposes. She decided not to take her spot in bed. She figured Gwen would think she took too much for granted. Not wanting to press her luck—after all, she was a spanking virgin—she sat straight up on the bench at the end of the bed. The door opened slowly, the dim light washing over Gwen's shapely body. Sternly she announced, "Go to bed, Jamie, now. I'll deal with you when I'm ready to." Jamie jumped at her tone, and even more disappointed than ever, she retreated to her side of the bed. She was beyond burning at this point. Even rejection made her desire flame out of control. She'd never felt this way before.

She both lavished in and hated every minute of it. She cried herself to sleep.

When Jamie awoke the next morning, Gwen was nowhere to be found. A crisp sealed envelope on the bathroom mirror was addressed to "Little Girl." Jamie slipped her finger under the seal and noticed her hands were trembling. The letter read:

My sweet little girl:

You are to call out today and not leave the house. You remain in your birthday suit all day, no matter what, no excuses. Order dinner in from Chianti's; I'll pick it up at 4 sharp. I'm not at work, so don't call me there. As a matter of fact, don't use the phone except to place the order. You can spend the day sunning out back, but no relief from the pool, and you're only permitted in the kitchen for beverages. Your breakfast and lunch are already set out in the spare room. (I thought you might do well to recall last night when you left me out of your party.) After you make the bed in our room, you're not allowed back in there until I come home tonight. You'll shower in the guest bathroom— all your things have been placed in there for you—and you're allowed two showers today, so choose when wisely. You will enter the bedroom at 4:15 P.M., light the candles, draw the drapes, and sit in the chair that you'll find has been placed in the corner. Don't bother looking now, because you won't see it. Kara has the extra key, and she'll be by some time during the day. You are not to see her, or talk to her, or she to you. So be smart about where you spend your time. She will be following some instructions I've given her. She'll leave when she's done.

I hope you can follow these directions to the letter, baby

girl—ultimately it's all for you my love.

Be good,
Gwen

Soaked and trembling with anticipation and curiosity, Jamie read the letter again. Then her curiosity got the better of her. She headed to the spare room, where she found a bowl of fruit and a big blueberry muffin on one plate and cheese, crackers, and yogurt with granola on another. Everything set out neatly on two trays, cloth napkins and utensils, too. Jamie felt like a Victorian mistress, minus the chambermaid. She spent her day lounging by the pool, indulging herself in what Gwen called self-gratification and wallowing in a little bit of annoyance at Gwen for involving Kara. Though it did intrigue her to think that Kara might be aware of the details in this adventure. Kara was Gwen's ex. They were a couple before Gwen and Jamie knew each other. Jamie knew the bedroom was one place they had no hindrances, and she resented Kara knowing about this.

At 2:30, Jamie heard a car in the driveway. She ran to the side porch to peek through the slats in the fence. It was Kara. Bags crinkling, keys jingling, no good hints of any kind there. She ran quickly back to the lounge chair. Wanting to appear nonchalant, she lay on her stomach pretending to read a magazine, in case Gwen had asked Kara to spy on her.

Twenty minutes had passed, and Kara was still there. She made a few more trips to the car. Finally Jamie heard the front door shut and the bolt turn; Kara got into her car and drove away.

Jamie was dying to see exactly what orders had been carried out. She went to take a look and was startled to find a note on the door right behind her. In big bold letters it read, KARA WILL BE COMING BACK SOMETIME TODAY TO MAKE SURE THAT NOTHING SHE DID WAS DISTURBED. DON'T DISAPPOINT ME. XOX

Jamie stood in horror. First, Kara had definitely seen her naked on the lounge chair! "Sleaze!" she snapped. Second, obviously Kara knew what was in store for her. That angered her! Mostly, it embarrassed her. It even turned her on, she had to admit. Angry or not, more or less she knew she had no control of this situation, and it was getting late. She needed to call and order the requested menu and take her shower. By the time she was finished, it was 4:10, and she wondered if Kara was really coming back. Convinced she wasn't, she smoothed on some baby oil and headed for the bedroom as directed.

She timorously opened the door, and there in the middle of the room was a small bistro table set for two. She dutifully went ahead and lit the various candles placed around the room, in the back of her mind still cursing Kara's part in all this. She pulled the drapes closed and noticed there was one chair by the table and the other by the door. Like a good little girl, she sat in the chair by the door. The seat was cool against her bare ass. She thought about how good it felt today not wearing a stitch of clothes. For the hundredth time today, her inner thighs quivered and her insides shuddered thinking about tonight. How would Gwen carry this out? Would they have dinner first, would they talk about technique? Jamie cringed when she realized this was something she knew absolutely nothing about but was dying to explore. She hoped in her heart that Gwen would continue to show complete control but offer her empathy and lenience, too.

The front door slammed, and Jamie jumped out of her skin. Flipping back her hair, she raced to take a quick last look in the mirror. She wanted to look innocent and sweet, so she had minimized the makeup to just clear lip gloss and mascara. All that sun today took care of her cheeks. She smiled approvingly at herself; she knew how to play this game. How her body tingled now, and she squirmed over the puddle she was making on the metal chair.

The doorknob turned. Gwen's silhouette was tall and lean. Jamie had always thought Gwen was striking, but she had never seen this domineering side of her. It brought out another aspect of her beauty.

"Hi, little girl. You have a nice day today?"

Jamie was grasping tightly either side of her seat. Poised to jump out, it seemed.

"Interesting, to say the least, actually."

"Well, good then. I hope you relaxed and thought about everything that will happen tonight." Coming closer to Jamie, she placed the take-out box on the bed. She squatted down in front of Jamie and laid her hands on Jamie's thighs. "Your body's shaking, baby," she said, leaning in for her hello kiss. "You're sure about this, right? I mean, you can change your mind, Jamie, you know this is all up to you."

Jamie responded, "Please don't ask me again, Gwen. Let's just do this, OK? I don't want to go backward after today."

"Good enough for me," Gwen said, and with that she stood up. "Put dinner on the table, then."

Jamie did as she was told and Gwen relished the visual. Gwen didn't speak through most of their meal, and Jamie knew not to speak first. She kept her answers short and feigned a bit of ambiguity about what was to come.

Intuitively, she knew Gwen got off on that. Suddenly, Gwen sat back from the table. "Get up, Jamie." As she stood, Gwen reached for her hand, pulling her down to kneel beside her. "This is what'll happen to you tonight. Are you ready?"

"Yes." Her eyes shone with fresh tears. "Yes."

"I have a blindfold for you if you want it." Jamie hadn't thought about it but now realized she would prefer it.

"Yes, yes, I do."

Pulling a black silk scarf from behind her, she stood up slowly, noticeably taller in her boots next to Jamie in her bare feet. "Face the wall, Jamie, spread your legs a little, and put your hands behind your back." Jamie's heart raced. Gwen saw the tears flowing down her cheeks, so having her face the wall was really to spare her from weakening. She tied the scarf around Jamie's eyes and led her to the bed. "You're not to speak at all. I want you to think about Laurie. I expect that tonight is the last time Laurie is in our bedroom. Clear?" Jamie nodded. "How did you hurt her, angel girl? Does it make you ache to recall her pain?" She positioned Jamie over her knees, and Jamie gasped and sobbed. Her body shook as she cried, her tears a combination of panic, guilt and release. Gwen traced her cheeks with her warm hand, and Jamie calmed down a little. Then Gwen raised her hand high, coming down on Jamie's ass with a fair amount of might. Jamie leaped forward and screeched. Gwen barely let her rest before she came down on her again. Four swift slaps followed the first two. Jamie's body rose, and Gwen pushed her down firmly. "Let her go now, Jamie. Let it go and know that you deserve to be loved and adored by me!" She paddled her with a steady rhythm for a few more seconds and then gently rubbed her reddened cheeks. Shifting her position for better grip, she let her fingers travel to Jamie's open pussy. Pinching her labia, she reminded Jamie of her "escapade for one" last night. "That wasn't nice, now, was it?" She laid four more hard smacks on Jamie's already sore bottom. Jamie squealed loudly, reaching back to soothe her cheeks. But Gwen was having none of that. Restraining her wrists, she added, "Next time I get to watch, at the very least.

"Now, show me you're sorry by devouring me completely while Kara clears the table."

Raging Hormones

TERRI GIANI

I worked the morning shift at the deli. This was the lesbian-owned deli up on the hill, with sandwiches on the menu named after famous feminists. Maybe it was because I was a staunch vegetarian, but the thought of a duck liver pâté sandwich ridiculously named the "Simone de Beauvoir" made me want to either puke or laugh hysterically. You pick. I had to hear wide-eyed yuppies say it earnestly every day, "a double decaf soy iced latte and a 'Seemoan doo Boovwah,' please. Do you have unsalted chips?" Such affectation made it hard to keep a straight face while I rang them up.

Down the hill was another story. It was 1989 in San Francisco. The earthquake hadn't happened yet. Amelia's, the old dyke bar on Valencia Street, was alive and well. The Artemis Café on Valencia and 23rd was always full of women. If you were a young, poor dyke musician like me, it was absolute paradise. You didn't need a phone back then; you just had to walk the street between 16th and 24th and you'd run into all your friends—some of them biking to work at the food co-op, some of them coming home from their AA meeting, some of them counting their dollars to go to the woman-owned sex toy store to buy lube and latex, some headed to check their mailbox to hear from some girl working at the music festival in Michigan.

I'd been licking my wounds because my longtime gal and I had split up a few months before. I had moved out of our beloved flat on Harrison Street and got a sublet with some straight chick close to Noe Valley.

So there I was trudging off to my job at the deli every morning at 5 A.M. It was just me and the speed freaks on the bus that snaked around the Potrero projects then lurched up to Fancy Land on top of the hill.

The cook and I spent every morning alone together for the first few hours of our shift. I washed lettuce and prepped sandwich fixings as she made lasagna. I bent over the meat slicer as she bent over bread dough. We flirted with each other and made each other laugh in those not-awake-yet hours. Rita was pregnant, noticeably pregnant, and married to some guy who used to be a pimp and a drug dealer. He was born-again now. She'd met him at City College. He didn't work. He was on disability for an old work injury. She had a daddy thing; he was older, and she was in love. But for all her talk about her man, she also liked women. Rita made certain I knew that she was bi, putting it into any conversation she could. I wanted to make sure she knew I was butch. I carried all her heavy boxes and buckets of food in and out of the walk-in cold storage. She always showed her appreciation by making me homemade cheese puffs and pouring me strong coffee.

I tried to make myself look busy but would sneakily check her out while she chopped onions or kneaded bread. With strands of hair hanging over her forehead, salty sweat droplets beaded up on her lip, and her tongue would occasionally trail up to snatch them. Her arms and chest and hands worked up a sweat, along with that baby, making body heat, causing her flashes. She'd catch my eye and smile with a lingering look. I swear, on those days there were extra onions chopped. I felt like Scott Baio with Beverly D'Angelo in some weird after-school movie. Her cleavage heaved as she kneaded the bread dough back and forth. Ample and swollen and overwhelming.

One morning I noticed with a mix of curiosity and extreme excitement that her nipples had created wet spots on her shirt. She was leaking. What do you say at a time like this? It's not like telling someone they have something in their teeth. I pretended not to notice and focused my eyes on her eyes or something else when we talked. I begged my mind to stop wandering. I went to the front counter and started counting money into the drawer. I was on the fives when she came up behind me and whispered in my ear, "Close your eyes and open your mouth."

I froze, stopped counting, a weird sound escaped my throat, and then I finally mustered up a smile and turned around to face her.

I tried to stay cool and act suave but my eyes immediately got locked on her nipples. Panicking, I slammed them shut. Without breathing, I opened my mouth. With my hands still holding bundled bills and my brain burning an image of a buxom pregnant babe with out of control nipples into me, I felt her finger slide slowly onto my bottom lip. I closed my lips around her finger and sucked it with my tongue. I kept my eyes closed as I heard her moan.

"Mmm, chocolate," I whispered, her finger still in my mouth. I opened my eyes and noticed the wet spots had gotten bigger. I let my eyes continue up to hers, which seemed very pleased.

I dropped the cash and grabbed her. We were kissing and

sucking and grabbing. Platters of cheese and pickles and stacks of paper cups went flying as I shoved them away with a frantic motion.

She grabbed at my ass and tried to put her hands up my shirt. I held her wrists and thrust her hands behind her back and bit her neck. If anyone was going to get done here, it was going to be her. It wasn't my usual thing to give it up so easy, especially to a married pregnant woman who was getting her rocks off seducing baby dykes at a lunch counter. I mean, she was acting like she really liked me, but I knew as I was stroking her very erect nipples that come tomorrow the pressure would be off and we could go back to being friends.

I wasn't big on casual sex, but I was no home wrecker and we weren't in love, so there was no guilt as I told her to follow me back into the kitchen, where I knew the butcher block was ready and waiting to be used for something besides slicing tomatoes.

I had her shorts down to her ankles and kept kissing her as we both pulled her underwear off. Then I saw her. I had never seen anything like her pussy and clit before. She was hugely swollen and slightly purplish-red. She was more than wet—she gushed. I had never had sex with a pregnant woman before, but I'd never had sex with a married woman either. I helped her get on the table and lean back before I put my fingers on her pussy. It didn't take much before she made it clear that she wanted me in her.

I leaned over to kiss and suck her nipples. A warm fluid seeped into my mouth. It was vaguely sweet and warm and kind of bland. I wasn't repulsed. But I wasn't especially turned on by it either. It just seemed like I would kiss and suck any other women's nipples, so why not hers? Rita absolutely loved it. She said "Yes, yes" and pushed my head into her chest. She bucked and moaned and pulled at me while I fucked her. Her pussy was burning hot and slicked my hand with her wetness. She felt open and thick all at the same time. I kept pumping and was soon up to four fingers. I wasn't sure whether I was hitting her uterus. I asked her if this was OK.

"It's more than OK, honey," she panted.

"I mean for the baby," I said apologetically, yet never once relenting.

"No, no, it's OK, don't worry. Everything is good for the baby. Just don't stop fucking me, please." She pounded back against my hand. "Yes, yes, yes."

With that, I fucked her and pinched her nipples till she screamed with a huge orgasm. Her body shuddered, and we were both drenched. I stood between her legs as she collapsed against me, catching her breath. After a few moments, we came out of our sex stupor, kissed sweetly, and I helped her down off the butcher block.

Rita got dressed and went to the bathroom. I washed my hands and doused the butcher block with diluted bleach water. Of course I didn't want my boss to smell our evidence, but also the virulent safe sex dogma of this time of plague doom and gloom had fed my already innate sense of germophobia. That expression about mixing your meat where you bake your bread, or however that goes, echoed in my head as I unlocked the front door and turned the OPEN sign around.

We had a system that if the morning crowd was bigger than normal we could ring a bell and whoever was on kitchen prep duty would come out to the counter to help. I rang the bell about five times that day, even though our morning rush was no rush at all.

I had named the customers in my head according to their orders. Macchiato Man came in as usual to pay in pennies. He always asked if our cups were made with hydrofluorocarbons or not. The first time I rang the bell Rita rushed out dramatically and bellowed at the 7 A.M. crowd to belly up to the bar. She winked at me and smiled as I yelled out to her that I needed a double mocha on the A-SAP. She put her hand on her hip and, right in front of the customer who was ordering, turned to me and waited till I looked up at her. Then she saucily inquired, "Do you need whipped cream with that?"

I smiled back and said "Most definitely," without asking the customer, who suddenly looked up from his paper with this "Sure, why not?" smile on his face.

I punched the buttons on the register and said, "Whipped cream? Everything is better with whipped cream, right, my man? Of course! More whipped cream!" I laughed out loud as I saw that the fives were in the 20s spot and there weren't any quarters at all.

Katie

A.D.R. Forté

Isn't it strange when you see someone at a distance or in passing and, for a moment, your heart stops, because in your bones you know that face, that posture. Then nobody is there, or a stranger turns to face you, and all you can do is walk away with a letdown emptiness, wondering if there was any meaning to the whole episode, or if it was just a creation of your own longing. That's how I feel about her, although I've long since relegated it to those cobwebby shelves. To bring her back into my life now would complicate things, but it's human nature to seek complication, right?

Nobody at my high school really ever knew about her. She was certainly unknown among my family and acquaintances. Nobody at all really knew what happened. Now when I talk about her as a lost conquest, some people believe me, some are shocked, and some can't give it any credibility. But that doesn't matter.

While I never considered myself remotely capable of interest in another female, I had friends who were unabashed about their preferences. Those of us, gay and straight, who found ourselves outside the norm—dubbed "goth" or "geek" or simply "weirdo"—convened to party on weekends.

Military towns don't offer much in the way of sophisticated partying, so we ended up driving an hour into the city to hit the club scene with the college crowd. I first met her on one of these outings. I admired her as one female does another, envied her silky red-brown hair and perfect smile, then forgot all about it.

We'd meet again at one of my friend Donna's parties.

"I'm inviting some people from P.U. You remember that one guy, and that other girl?" Donna loved to ramble on about her proposed guest list.

I nodded without the faintest recollection. "Yeah, um-hmm."

"You were talking to her...remember? The redhead? She's a junior and she's really, really hot!" Donna was one of the unabashed.

"I don't think I was drunk, but no, I still don't recall."

"Well, anyway, you'll meet her again. She's so nifty!"

Since Donna was the expert judge on who was nifty, I took her word for it and left it at that. When I got to the party, Donna ran up to hug me and, looking stunning behind her in an unimaginably tight sweater, stood the redhead I had talked to: Katie. Finally, my backsliding memory came up with a café on Sixth Street well after 2 A.M. and a little group of those of us unable to sleep before daybreak, whiling away a Saturday night. What we had talked about was beyond me, but I remembered that intelligent, attractive face, and her smile. A natural, generous smile I couldn't help but return. Still, she was just a newfound friend, and even if she was a lesbian, that was irrelevant—since I was straight. My body had no reason to respond to her in any way, and it didn't.

Still, the power of suggestion is amazing. Even looking

back, it's still hard to determine the workings of my sub-conscious. We talked, watched TV, and socialized together as if we'd known each other all along. That wasn't strange; familiarity has always been easy for me. But she finally asked, "So, you aren't into girls at all? You've never been with one?" The way she looked at me: I'd seen guys look at me like that, I'd looked at guys like that, and I knew what that look meant. I saw the concealed hopefulness and inter-est, the gamble she prayed would fall in her favor.

The transition came and went without even a minute wasted wrangling over the decision. Maybe the time spent with my open-minded friends had done its work, or maybe those who argue for genetics are right and it was there all along waiting for when I was ready. I've spent hours rea-soning about it since, but right then it was the work of a heartbeat.

"No, I haven't ever. I don't know why, though, because I don't really have anything against it. It might be fun."

I was flirting with another woman for the first time in my life. I couldn't believe it came out so simply. I noticed the tightness of her sweater, the curve of her leg folded under her on the sofa next to me. I noticed she was beauti-ful, and it excited me. I smiled; she offered a dazzling one in return and put her hand over my own in my lap.

She kissed me. I had no idea how to proceed—although, God knows, I was no stranger to the art—but once she had broken that ice, I knew immediately where I wanted to touch her, how to hold her. Around us, couples were find-ing each other, and we were part of that.

Katie bit my neck, and it was an erotic shock. I hadn't expected that much pleasure, like a giant wave breaking right above me in the surf. Our legs got tangled somehow, and the heat between our thighs pulsed and pressed together through our jeans while we kissed and reached out with hesitant hands. The excitement of a new and until now forbidden sensation far outweighed the thrill of anything I'd done before. And when she slid soft fingers inside me— right there on the sofa—I came until my head swam.

After that I spent more time in the city than I'd ever planned. She would drive up to get me on Fridays. Sometimes she would go with me to the high school football games. We'd cuddle under our blanket, with Donna and her girl under theirs next to us. It was a good feeling. The guys I knew would come over to talk after the game, and they'd gaze at her like blood-frenzied sharks circling prey. I admit I'm not above gloating—I'd grin at the futility of their attempts. Poor misguided souls.

Katie and I would then go back to her apartment to stay up all night talking, caressing, exploring with hands and tongues until, exhausted and satisfied, we'd curl up and fall asleep.

Our relationship was perfect, but it was never serious. Only now I wonder if she had wanted it to be. I told her from the start I wasn't into commitment. Boyfriend today, new boyfriend tomorrow, and that's how I felt about all relationships. She seemed OK with that: We had a great friendship and great sex, what more did we need? And I still had my eye on guys, of course. I left her free to look and touch wherever she wished. Anyway, we lived so far apart from each other. She accepted the rules and never pushed for more. Well, we all have regrets in life, and whatever I missed out on, there are still certain moments that stay sharp in my memory.

One is the first night I fucked her, the first time we really made love. Though it had been only a little more than two months, it seemed like we'd been lovers forever. The cold and rainy February had given me a bad case of fretful depression. We'd gotten back to her place late that Friday, but neither of us was tired. The frustrations of the past week had produced a lot of pent-up nervous energy, and we were barely into her room before we were kissing—and tugging impatiently at each other's clothes.

"Wait, wait wait," she gasped, and turned to rummage in her closet for her box of goodies. We'd played with toys from its delightful depths before: clamps, teasers, vibrators, all that a woman's heart could desire. But she ignored those and tugged out a black vinyl harness with a thick, silicone phallus attached.

"Seven inches!" she bragged. "Do you have any idea how to use one of these?"

I'd never even seen a dildo before, but I had a sudden intense desire to drive it into her. It was a lovely, intimate, obscene feeling, and I'm sure she read my mind.

"I haven't the foggiest idea what to do with one, but I'm sure I'll figure it out."

Laughing, she threw it at me and followed, stripping off her bra and panties on the way to the bed. Her hair was all over the place and so was mine. It brushed our cheeks and got in the way while we tried to get the dildo secured around my waist. The sensation was exciting, maddening, balanced by awkward fingers and clumsy efforts. We giggled the entire time, and to an outside observer it was probably the least erotic of scenes. But to me it was thrilling. Her eyes were shining, and when at last it was on and comfortable, she practically dragged me to the middle of the bed.

I straddled her on her back, trying frantically to keep my

hair out of my face, cope with the strangeness of the strap-on and the friction of the thong between my legs, and most of all please her at the same time. I so badly wanted it to be incredible for her that for once my own satisfaction wasn't even a concern. For a wild moment I thought, *I don't believe I'm really doing this!* Then all I could concentrate on was getting that dildo between her thighs.

She was ready, as excited and unsure as I was, although all her concern was for me. I put my trust in my instincts and slid two fingers into her. She was hot and pulsing already, and I slicked her moisture over her outside lips. Her hands were busy alternately stroking my breasts and her own, and it was hell just to concentrate with her nails merciless on my aroused nipples. Somehow the gods were with me and I thrust true, almost full into her. She gasped and grabbed my hips to pull me closer. Thrusting, missing, then laughing, I finally filled her up with my tool. Right then I understood penis envy; I wanted to feel her while I was inside. There was that one short moment of emptiness, of dissatisfaction. But then the look of dizzy pleasure on her face was enough for me, and I stretched full across her so that our nipples kissed and I could look down into her pretty, mascara-smudged eyes while we did this incredible, insane thing.

I was doing my best to pay full attention to her, to keep my rhythm, to gauge every expression as she squirmed under me to find the most pleasurable position. But the pressure of the thong rubbing on my clit and my vulva with every fraction of movement I made was driving me crazy. I was moaning softly, and she whispered between thrusts for me to come when she did. Her own cries grew harsher, and I gritted my teeth, lay full against her, and ground my hips into hers.

She strained upward, adding the force of her thrust to the pressure on my clit. The sensation was like was hanging on the edge of a roller coaster about to plunge downward, the instant before hitting the water after a dive. Then the energy rushed out of us in endless spasms. I was lost in this feeling and didn't realize what she was doing, when suddenly her fingers pushed into me, past our taut thighs, past the leather thong of the strap-on, finding me where I was most vulnerable. I let my head fall onto her shoulder. It felt like my every muscle turned to water as I came again.

I'd been on top, the one fucking her, but she was utterly in control. It didn't matter what she asked, I'd have done anything to please her. We didn't say anything for a long time as we untangled ourselves, turned off the lights, tidied the blankets, and snuggled under them. I felt uncharacteristically tongue-tied and shy. Nothing we'd done before had been so violent or intense, and the afterglow had never been so intimate.

We lay together, still getting our breath back and listening to the Celtic CD I'd put in, struck with inspiration, or maybe emotion. I don't know what it was, but I turned and began to kiss her. I kissed her mouth and her neck, then moved lower, caressing her breasts and nipples with my hand, then my tongue. I wanted this to be slow, gentle, and perfect. I wanted to remember at least this one night for as long as I was capable of coherent recollection. She was so incredibly beautiful, and I wasn't envious—I didn't compare myself to her, I just adored her. I kissed her thighs, still moist from our earlier tumble, and nudged them gently apart. I knelt between her legs and found every inch of her with my lips, pulling back every now and then to study her face and to run my fingers over her legs and stomach. I toyed with her, my tongue inside her, my hands pinching her swollen nipples until she told me to turn over. I refused. I wanted to worship her.

We made a graceful, sensual sculpture in the near dark: languid, arched limbs, tangled hair, muscles tensed to every sensation. I never faltered in my gentle ministrations until her head fell back and she gasped, tightening her grasp on my shoulders. Sweet liquid gushed over my tongue, and I didn't lose a bit of her. I savored every drop and every second of her climax. I crawled up to the pillow beside her. She reached out fumblingly to touch me. Everything she was feeling showed in her touch. Then I let the syrupy darkness claim my exhausted body.

There were other times after that night, times when the whole world ceased to exist because I was with Katie. Scenes played through my head whenever we weren't together and made me soak my panties. It wasn't just the sex. It was the way we could be violent and cruel, or tender and sensual to the point of tears.

There were the guys I half-heartedly dated, and there was the mild experimenting with Katie and other girls, but being alone with her was what I wanted most. With the wisdom of hindsight I think she was the real reason I never lost my other "virginity" that year we were together. To have gotten laid would have felt like an infidelity.

Be that as it may, even as I got involved with her, I lost her. My own life was a mess and I felt ashamed to be with her, as if in my miserable state I had no right to screw things up for her. As months went by, I saw less of her, and the gulf inevitably widened. I found excuses not to go to the city, and after graduation I avoided those friends who knew us both. I told myself that Katie couldn't really see anything in me, that she had to be busy with her own life, that it was all over and done with.

I took a perverse satisfaction in my loneliness, in the ache of not seeing her, not touching her. I tortured myself with wondering where she was, what she was thinking. Sometimes in the midst of depressed, lonely, confused weeks I longed to call her. I wandered around the house, avoiding the phone, prodding and turning over my emotions until I had fully scared myself out of it. Sometimes I hoped she would call, but she didn't.

Finally I just locked it up as a happy time I could not return to. I let Katie go, except for the occasional daydream and the fantasies that never left. In that other world all the might-have-beens work out. In reality, other people have come and gone in my life. But Katie was my first real taste of love. And I don't suppose I will ever forget.

Rock Star Spanking

RACHEL KRAMER BUSSEL

I forget exactly how Suzette and I met, at some lesbian event or another, but I was totally attracted to her from the first. She was gorgeous, tall and lean with a fabulous smile and an even better laugh. She had short curls that clung to her head and a boyish but sexy figure. She talked animatedly, whether about her favorite book or a great new club, and I was quite smitten.

We went on one wild date and wound up kissing wildly on the dance floor, her biting my neck and me bending back for more. I loved being with her, running my hands up and down her body, marveling that she liked me too. We went back to her place and continued making out but didn't go much further, saving sex for another night.

The next week she told me that she'd never been to a play party and that there was an upcoming women's party she wants to attend. We made plans to go the next weekend. The truth is, I was surprised she'd never been to one. Not that I was ultra-experienced, but I'd been going to parties in the dyke S/M scene for a few months, and while I hadn't yet worked up the courage to actually play at one of them, I'd gotten to know the local players and what the scene was like. Though I'd been to a few events at the dungeon where this party would be held, I was still not sure what to expect;

each one had a different crowd and atmosphere.

We walked in the door, me clutching her hand tightly, proud to have her as my date. We chatted with some friends we knew and watched a few scenes. I held her hand and stood close behind her as we watched a woman tied up against the wall being severely beaten as the crowd stood by silently. I squeezed her hand at the most intense moments.

Shortly thereafter, a buzz arose in the hallway that a famous dyke rock star was at the party. Soon enough, we were introduced to her. She walked over to a group of us and said, "Hi, I'm Alex" (not her real name). Bold, direct, in-your-face. She stuck her hand out, and we shook it. (Later I overheard her introduce herself to a young woman who simply replied, "I know.") She greeted us with her buzz cut, angry tattoos, and piercing gaze. I shook her hand and smiled weakly, unsure of what to do with all the energy beaming at me.

Later, I left Suzettte in the food room and wandered off with another friend to explore a small play room. We found a pulley and stood examining it, having fun. "How does this work? Do you strap your wrists into it?" asked my friend.

"Let's find out," I said, offering my own wrists to be tested (I later found out that it's used to suspend you by your ankles). She struggled to get the restraints tightly enough around my wrists while I looked up nervously.

Though I am into pain in some situations, being suspended there was not a pleasant kind of pain. I began right away to feel a dull ache in my wrists and felt nervous hanging there in the air. I was about to ask her to let me down when I looked over and saw a group of girls watching us. Then who walks in but Alex, all calm and macho. She walked right up to me and, with a sadistic gleam in her eye, said, "What do you want to do now?" I was suddenly light-headed and uncertain. While she was totally hot, I'm not usually that much of an exhibitionist (some would protest this, but at least in this situation I wasn't), and my wrists were very much starting to hurt. Feeling like a total fool, I said, "I'd like to get down now."

"Really?" she asked with a smirk, then she helped untie me. After I'd been safely untied, I took a seat on the floor with the other voyeurs, but Alex was still eager for some play. She asked for volunteers from the group of young women staring in rapt attention, and promptly got one. That girl's scene made me glad I wasn't up there, as Alex tapped her lightly, then more heavily, with canes and paddles and hands.

I retired to the food room to eat and drink and chat with some friends, still wound up from the unexpected excite-ment. Suddenly, Suzette came running breathlessly into the room. She moved toward me, took my hand and said, "Alex is going to spank me now. I thought you might want to know and come watch." Of course I did! I abandoned the cheese and crackers and raced behind her to the same room I'd inadvertently gotten strung up in. A much bigger crowd sat watching.

I marched with Suzette up to the front of the room, where she lay down on a bench alongside the wall. I sat near her feet while Alex stood above her. "Are you ready?" Alex asked her.

"Yes, ma'am."

With that, Alex began delivering Suzette's spanking, using strong and forceful whacks that quickly reddened her skin. "Is that too much?" Alex asked after a series of particularly strong blows.

"No, it's perfect, I love it," Suzette said, wiggling her flawless ass and smiling as she rested her head against the bench. The spanking continued, while I got wetter and wetter. I didn't know who I wanted to be in this situation, I was totally into watching Suzette, but certainly enjoyed the pleasures of having a well-spanked ass myself. Alex paused and sent her piercing gaze back into me, seeming to both ask permission to fuck Suzette, and to take it. She reached for my hand and placed it over one of Suzette's glowing ass cheeks, letting me feel the heat of her handiwork. I smiled at the intensity, admiring the waves of warmth emanating from her ass, marveling at how a few minutes of vigorous slaps could generate as much heat, momentarily at least, as a sunburn—but a sunburn never felt so good!

Alex snapped on a latex glove and lubed up her gloved hand. "That's what these are here for, right?" she asked, mostly to herself, as she began to work a finger into Suzette's wet cunt. Suzette moaned and wriggled against Alex as Alex continued to work her pussy. My eyes were on Alex's hand, as it moved rapidly back and forth, and fucked Suzette brilliantly. She'd worked herself up to four fingers when her thumb began playing with Suzette's asshole, then easily slipped inside. Suzette looked like she was in heaven, and I smiled to myself.

I sat watching, thrilled and turned on at being both a voyeur and a participant. I stared intently as Alex plumbed Suzette's asshole, watched as Suzette squirmed in bliss. Her red-hot ass wiggled and bobbed. I wanted to lean down and lay my head on her ass, but instead I just kept looking, feeling myself get wet at this intimate display. Even with a room full of people watching, it felt intimate and special.

For her first play party, she did pretty well.

Unexpected Pleasures

MARIA V. CILETTI

"I haven't had a date in over six months," I complained to my ex-husband, now–best friend as we sat nursing a couple of beers on the back porch of what in a previous life was "our home."

"Speaking of dates, I need one for next Saturday," Ken said.

"What for?"

"One of the rookies from the department is getting married. The wedding is next Saturday, and the reception is at the Metroplex. It starts at 7, are you free?"

"Gee, I'll have to check my calendar." I flipped though my imaginary date book. "Yeah, I guess I'm free."

Our divorce was not your typical parting; I left my husband of nearly 10 years to be with a woman. As tragic as that may sound, Ken took it pretty well, considering what a blow it must have been to his male ego. He tells me that he came to the realization that my falling in love with another woman was the one thing with which he couldn't compete.

Although Ken and I have been divorced for almost five years, we've managed to maintain a close friendship and occasionally step in for each other to serve as a date, or in my case a "beard," for wedding or other special occasions.

Being a police captain's wife who jumps the heterosexual

fence to play on the pink team had the rumor mills spinning out of control. Usually it's the cop who cheats, and everyone looks the other way; in our case it was the quiet, unassuming wife, and the police ranks were running with it.

I have to admit, when I heard the awful things people were saying about me I was devastated, but looking back, even though it was one of the most painful decisions I ever had to make, I know I made the right one. I needed to be true to who I really am: a woman who loves other women.

I met my first love, Regan, at the nursing home where we both worked. Regan was a new grad, and as the charge nurse, I was assigned to her orientation. We became fast friends, and on a sticky summer night, on the floor of my living room, Regan and I became more. It was awkward and magnificent, and that's when it hit me that I had finally found who I really was.

In the winter of 1989, after a prolonged emotional tug-of-war between my husband and Regan, I finally got up the courage to leave. Six months after my divorce was final, Regan eloped to West Virginia with the maintenance man from the nursing home. Life really sucks sometimes.

Saturday night arrived, and so did I—on Ken's doorstep wearing a black sleeveless sheath dress and black patent leather pumps.

"Jesus, if you would have dressed like this when we were married, maybe…"

"Never mind," I interrupted. "I'll be waiting in the car."

Ken and I entered the hall and were greeted by the groom, a strapping 26-year-old rookie who obviously had an intimate ongoing relationship with a universal gym, and his bride, a petite blond computer programmer from

Connecticut. Ken placed his hand in the small of my back and guided me through the receiving line and out into the sea of white linen–draped round tables. The room was packed, but we got lucky and found two seats at an already crowded table near the buffet. Relief swept over me when I realized I didn't recognize any of the people at the table.

Ken worked with all of the guys we were sitting with. Most of them were quite young, and so were their spouses. Ken introduced me to his coworkers, and I nodded and smiled politely, secretly yearning for a gin and tonic.

Ken and a few of the guys from our table sauntered over to the bar, leaving me with the other women. The conversation included the usual childcare highlights, work issues, etc. The things most straight women talk about when they get together. Flashbacks of another time flooded my memory, and that old uneasy feeling in the pit of my stomach returned with a vengeance. I wasn't like these women. I had nothing in common with them—at least I didn't think I did.

I listened to their chitchat, telepathically trying to tell Ken to hurry up at the bar and bring me my drink. It was only 7:30 and I was already bored out of my mind. I stood up and excused myself from the table to head off to the ladies room. I didn't have to go, but if I had to listen to one more story about the trials and tribulations of potty training, I was going to kill myself.

"Mind if I join you?" came from Becky, one of the younger officer's wives.

Before I could answer, she stood up and grabbed her red sequined cocktail purse.

"No, not at all," I lied, and I headed for the rest room with Becky in tow.

The rest room was spaciously elegant. Gleaming black

and white marble floors and counters with gold fixtures. Full-length mirrors adorned the walls and plush maroon couches lined the far wall of the powder area. Becky slipped into one of the bathroom stalls, while I fumbled around with the contents of my purse. I usually don't carry a purse, but there was nowhere in my dress to put a wallet. I applied some lip gloss and messed around with my hair, which is so short a hurricane couldn't blow it out of place.

Becky emerged from the stall, looking gorgeous in her red sequined dress, and approached the counter, where I was still fumbling. She leaned over the sink to wash her hands, giving me full view of her lovely cleavage in the reflection of the mirror. She turned off the faucet, looked up into the mirror, and caught me staring.

Horrified, I stood there frozen.

"Do you find these events as boring as I do?" she said with a slow, secret smile as she snapped open her purse and pulled out a tube of lipstick.

"Huh? Oh, yes…" Suddenly the room was too hot and my knees felt weak.

I looked away but found it hard to keep my eyes off her as she applied a fresh coat of red lipstick to her lush lips. She had a wealth of dark hair that hung in long graceful curves over her shoulders. She obviously kept a regular schedule at the gym as well.

"I didn't know you and the captain were back together again," Becky said to her reflection.

"Oh, we're not… We go out sometimes, just as friends," I stammered.

"That's so nice you can be friends after your divorce."

"Yes, it is," I answered, still rummaging in my purse, trying to pull myself together.

I was finally able to compose myself long enough to walk back to the table without passing out from embarrassment. Becky walked ahead of me, her ample bottom swaying in the confines of her form-fitting dress. The girl had a great body. I will give her that much. Thankfully, Ken was back at our table with my drink. I definitely needed it, more than ever.

"You look like you've just seen a ghost," Ken said as I dropped down into the chair next to him.

"I'll tell you later," I whispered.

I took a big swallow of my drink, and the world started to feel like a better place. Then all of the sudden, a hand came to rest on my stocking-covered knee. Annoyed, I turned to tell Ken to quit it, but it wasn't him in the seat next to me. My body stiffened.

The soft, delicate hand stirred slightly, slowly, now caressing my knee and inner thigh. A shudder passed through me and I felt the familiar heat spread through my groin. To the others at the table, Becky appeared to be sitting demurely, both hands in her lap, looking off into the crowd, minding her own business.

Slowly, Becky inched her cool hand higher on my leg. I tossed back my drink, finishing it in one big gulp, then bolted up from my chair. "I need another drink. Anybody want anything?"

To my relief, Ken was standing at the bar. I squeezed in next to him.

"Are you all right?" he asked.

"No. I need another drink."

"What's the matter? You're a wreck."

"Cunningham's wife is putting the moves on me."

"What?"

"Jim Cunningham's wife...Becky...flirted with me in the ladies room and at the table she had her hand on my knee."

"Get out of here! Why would she do something like that?"

I glared at him and he got the message.

"Oh, yeah...no...you don't think...?"

"It may have been a while, but I still know when a woman is coming on to me."

"I don't believe it."

I told him about the events in the bathroom and at the table.

"Holy shit, what are you going to do?"

"What do you mean what am I going to do? Nothing. I'm not going to be a muff-diving instructor for some curious straight chick who wants to test the water. Been there, done that, and had my heart handed to me in shreds. No, thank you. I'm not getting involved."

"Where's your sense of adventure, Mina? Oh, give the girl a thrill."

"Are you nuts! Jesus, I'm so alone here."

"Hey, maybe Cunningham and I can watch."

"Oh, shut up, Ken. You're a lot of help."

I ordered another gin and tonic and drank it standing at the bar.

Just when I started to feel better, Becky came up behind me. "I didn't mean to make you uncomfortable," she said. I could feel her warm breath on my neck. It sent chills through me.

Becky pushed her way closer to the bar to stand beside me. She put her hand on my arm.

"I just thought...that we were the same," she said.

"What gave you that impression?"

"I heard why you and the Captain split up. That's the same thing I have been struggling with all my life."

As much as I didn't want to, I heard the sincerity in her voice. I turned to look at her. Her eyes were dark and unfathomable. My heart beat faster.

"Becky, this isn't something to mess around with."

She hung her head, and her sadness seemed to fill the bar area.

"Hey, I didn't mean to put you down. It's just that...when I finally decided this is what I wanted, it was tough. I hurt a lot of people in the process, and I got hurt, too. It's no picnic."

"Couldn't we just go out some time to talk? I don't know where to go to meet other women...I don't know anyone else who has been in this position."

I felt my defenses begin to weaken. "Jimmy's on afternoon turn this week. How about Wednesday night?"

"Sure. Wednesday will be fine."

"Great!" she said.

Becky peeled a cocktail napkin from the top of a stack on the bar, scribbled her phone number on it, and handed it to me. I reluctantly did the same. She went back to the table, and I ordered another drink.

Wednesday night came. Becky appeared at my apartment in a pair of jeans that left not very much to the imagination and a crisp, white oxford shirt.

"This really means a lot to me. Thank you," Becky said as we got into my car and headed for Cleveland and the only women's bar I knew of in Northeastern Ohio.

"So, have you talked to your husband about your feelings?" I asked, breaking the uncomfortable silence.

"No, I don't think he would understand."

"I see."

Silence again enveloped the car. "Have you ever..."

She turned toward me. "Ever what?"

"Have you ever...acted on your feelings? You know...with another..."

"No, never." Becky stared out the passenger window.

"Are you sure you want to do this?"

"Yes. I'm tired of living my life under others' expectations."

"OK, but I have to warn you that this might be scary. There will be all kinds of women there."

"I was hoping you would say that." She gave me a mischievous smile.

"Really. I remember my first time in a gay bar. I was scared to death."

"So how did you get over it?"

"It took time. I had to keep reminding myself that, like a lot of things in life, people fall on different points of the spectrum, and the more people I met and the more friends I made, the more comfortable I became with who I am."

We arrived at the bar at 9:30. Women of all shapes, sizes, and colors were trickling in through the front entrance, whose enormous oak door separated two worlds: In the first, you had to be who everyone expected you to be, and in the second, you could be who you actually were. As we reached the door, the ID checker asked to see our licenses, which made me laugh. I hadn't been carded in 10 years. The room was dim and smelled of beer and Sebastian cologne. Becky grabbed my arm as we entered.

"What are you doing?" I asked.

"Nothing, just a little nervous," she said.

"If you hold on to me like that, people will think we're

together, and you might lose out on hooking up with someone."

She smiled with an air of pleasure.

All I could do was shake my head. I ignored her response and led her farther into the bar. Heads turned as we passed. Becky was an attractive woman, but I am sure some of the attention was due to her being "fresh meat."

The wooden dance floor had seen better days and was currently vacant. Not all that much of a surprise, because the music sounded like someone banging on a steel pipe with a crescent wrench.

We found two seats on the other side of the bar. I ordered our drinks: gin and tonic for me, cosmopolitan for her. As Becky pulled a 20 from her purse, I laughed. Nobody in this joint carried a purse.

After the second round of drinks, the hand games resumed. Becky rested her fingers on my knee and slowly dragged her nails up the inseam of my jeans. I couldn't deny the spark I felt at the prospect of making love to this beautiful woman, but it just wouldn't be right...right?

"Becky. What are you doing?"

Her eyes were moist as they searched mine for some hint of what I was feeling. "Don't you find me attractive?"

"Yes, of course I do, but..."

"But what? Not your type? Not pretty enough or thin enough?"

"No, Becky, you're beautiful. Definitely the most beautiful woman in here. It's just that you're married. I've been there before. It sucks..."

"Did it stop you from finding out who you really are?"

"No, it didn't, but it's not something to take lightly. Doing this will change your whole life."

"I want that same chance. Is that so terrible?"

A slow song was playing. I got off my barstool. "OK, then," I said, extending my hand to her. " Would you like to dance?"

Becky's face lit up. She took my hand and hopped from her seat. Her hand trembled as I led her to the dance floor, which was not so abandoned now. I slipped my arms around her slim waist, holding her close and swaying to the music. She wasn't sure where to put her arms at first. I lifted them gently, easing her arms over my head and around my neck. She held me tight, and I could feel every part of her. Breasts, belly, hips, all pressed into me.

I felt myself slipping, becoming lost in her softness. I moved my hands up and gently caressed her back, surprised to discover she wasn't wearing a bra. She pulled me closer and breathed in my ear, which sent shivers through me. Then the music ended and we stood face to face.

I kissed her. Her lips were soft and warm. My tongue searched her mouth and she went limp in my arms. "Let's get out of here," I said.

Once inside the car, we couldn't keep our hands off each other. I wasn't sure I could hold off until we got back to my place.

The entire way home previews of her naked body flashed through my mind, fueling my passionate fire. We held hands all the way, then burst through the doorway of my apartment, landing on the couch in the stillness of the apartment. Our kisses grew fervent; I couldn't wait any longer and attacked the buttons on her shirt. Her soft, full breasts with their erect pink nipples seemed to ache for my touch.

"My God, Becky, you are so beautiful," I gasped.

She smiled, her face basking in the glow of the lone

streetlight, which shone in through the living room window. I bent down and kissed her neck, her collarbone, her breasts. Her body arched beneath me and she gasped in sweet agony. I caressed her swollen nipple with my tongue, as her breathing accelerated. She stretched out beneath me, in agonized pleasure. My tongue left a damp trail from her ribs to her flat stomach. I unbuttoned the top button of her jeans and I eased down the zipper, then—in one motion—removed her jeans and panties.

Her pussy was lush, dark, and swollen. She spread her legs wide, inviting me in. I lowered my face just inches from her pussy, inhaled her musky scent, and felt the throb in my own groin. I blew a gentle stream of air over her clit and she immediately thrust up her crotch. I pulled my mouth away and she cried out in frustration. I rubbed my cheek over the silky skin of her belly and inner thighs. A low moan escaped her lips as my tongue made contact.

Her fingers twisted in my hair as she tried to direct the attention I gave her pussy. When she guided me to her clit, I retracted my tongue.

"Fuck me. Oh, please, fuck me! Make me come." Her whisper was raspy with anticipation.

I placed the tip of my index finger at the opening of her sopping wet hole, gently massaging it. She squirmed, trying to impale herself, but to no avail.

"You want this inside of you...don't you," I said, now circling the opening of her cunt with my finger.

"Oh, yes...Oh, please...put it in..."

I slid my finger in a littler farther, and she moaned with relief. Then I stopped. Her body was still, but her pussy pulsed against my finger. My own jeans were soaked clean through.

She squirmed again, trying to push my finger in deeper.

I finally gave up and shoved it in all the way. She moaned loudly, and I was beginning to worry the neighbors might hear. Her cunt was hot, wet, and overflowing as I slowly pushed three fingers in and out of her.

"Faster!" she gasped. "Please, go faster."

I ignored her and continued my slow, rhythmic pace. When I felt she couldn't take any more, I lowered my face to her pussy and with one long, wet stroke, licked her swollen clit. She exploded instantly, raising her hips high off the couch and almost giving me whiplash. I continued to lick and suck her clit until she pushed my face away.

"Enough! Enough!" She curled up in a ball in the corner of the couch, drenched in sweat.

I slid up behind her, stroked her damp hair, and held her close. She slowly returned to consciousness, her face glowing with a lazy smile. She looked up at me, a mixture of love and lust in her eyes.

"Are you sure this is what you want?" I asked.

"Mm-hmm," she murmured, and drowsily closed her eyes.

I took her hand, gently kissed it, then placed it on my own throbbing crotch. Her eyes popped open as she felt the heat radiate through my soaking wet jeans.

"Yes, but are you ready for this?"

Pawn Takes Queen

SYDNEY LARKIN

I didn't want to tell her what I had been thinking.

The night before, Jody and I had been watching a childhood-indulgent screening of *The Muppet Movie* in Kellie's dorm room. I rubbed Jody's shoulders during the first part of the film. Then we took a break, and she told me to move over so she could lie next to me on the bed. I did, my attention aroused (along with other parts of me), but I remained reserved because I knew if she got any indication of my feelings it would take us back to harder days. She lay in front of me, on her side, her back to me.

It was uneventful at first. She reached behind her back, searching for my hand. She found it, grasped it in her own, and gently placed it on top of her abdomen. I thought nothing of it. Her hand held mine, and I was in a state of complete contentment.

And then her hand moved.

She lifted it to her face to brush her hair out of her eyes, and I found my hand in the sensitive area of her breasts. I wasn't sure what to do. My body screamed for me to caress them, but my mind reminded me that she probably wouldn't react well to that. After all, she was straight, and she had been clear that she wasn't interested in anything beyond friendship. But, being the optimistic person that I was, I knew there was always a possibility, so I moved my hand in such a manner that it lightly stroked her breast.

She made no attempt to remove it from that area of forbidden territory.

And I was aptly confused.

I just did not know what to think of the entire situation. We were exceptionally intimate; the honesty between us, even when painful, was the most profoundly close thing I had ever experienced. Of course, I also found her extraordinarily beautiful and irresistibly charming. When she walked into a room my heart beat faster and the air felt heavier.

High school had been a cruel social experience. I had been completely closed off emotionally in general, made worse by the fact that I was barely out to myself to begin with. College had promised camaraderie, community, and the possibility of meeting an intellectual equal. I found that in Jody, and much more.

But most importantly, she drew me out of myself, and I loved who I was when I was with her. All of this brought me to the conclusion that she was the ideal person for me, save her wrong sexual orientation. Which is why I was so bewildered by the contact she allowed that evening.

On the other hand, we had been fairly physical all day. She had come over to me while I was sitting in my desk chair and promptly sat down on my lap. Not that I minded—quite the contrary. I would have done anything to be close to this woman.

But her actions that night—or rather, lack thereof—allowed all of the emotions I'd pushed aside to resurface. I was indeed in love with her, and had been for quite some time. There had been a rift in our relationship during the first few months following my confession, so my best judgment was to engage in the fine art of repression. Part of me wanted to write off her behavior as just something she was comfortable with. The rest of me could not let it lie.

My sister was visiting me at school for a few days. She had gone back to my room to help Kellie, who was typing a paper on my computer. I went back to my room and got out the vodka I had smuggled into the building in a water bottle, thinking it would be nice to be a bit intoxicated, to get my mind off of what had just happened. I drank a little, and my tongue became loose as the alcohol quickly invaded my body. I told my sister and Kellie about what had just transpired.

"Can I make a really crass comment? I just want to fuck her brains out!" I exclaimed. They both laughed and suggested I might have a chance, but that I shouldn't say anything for fear of scaring Jody.

I went to sleep, my mind wandering to thoughts of Jody in my arms. I woke up the next morning to vague memories of very erotic dreams. The day went on as usual. It was a Tuesday, and Jody and I wrote our usual notes in Eggenschwiler's class. Egg, as we called him, was notorious for bizarre, off-the-cuff remarks that made our note writing much more entertaining. "The bakkie is a recreational vehicle—an RV—for pleasure only. The other car in the driveway. Like a whore: for pleasure only; the other woman…in the driveway." I think it was around the time that Egg was drawing a parallel between a jeep and a prostitute that I got up the courage.

"What should I do?" I wrote.

"Follow your heart," she replied. I felt a nervous tingling in my stomach. Of course, she was referring to something else entirely, my problem with Laurie, a woman who had expressed interest in me, and my ambivalent feelings about the whole matter.

Later that afternoon, Jody and I sat talking in my room. She knew something was eating me. "What are you thinking?"

I didn't want to tell her.

I tried to avoid the question, which resulted only in pissing her off. Finally, I could not hold it in any longer. I quietly asked her if she remembered anything out of the ordinary happening the night before in Kellie's room. She did not—so I tried to drop the subject. But she was relentless , so I broke down and told her everything I was feeling. I related my side of the story of how my hand had ended up on her breast, and how I didn't know what her not moving it meant.

"Have you ever considered the fact that perhaps I have gotten more comfortable with you physically in the past months because the tension is no longer there?"

I replied with a yes, that this was what I had expected. I also expressed my conflicting opinions about telling her, how I didn't want to cross any boundaries unintentionally and make her uncomfortable, and yet, if I brought it to her attention, perhaps she would reconsider letting me be close to her. She understood, and said that pulling away from me was not on her mind.

We began to discuss my feelings for her, a subject that was all too familiar to us both. I was afraid she would tire of hearing about them. I told her how much power she had over me, and she said that she knew this. In fact, we talked about how she could seduce me at any moment just for fun, knowing I would not resist, and how that would be the ultimate betrayal.

Eventually, sex came up in the conversation, and Jody complained about how horny she'd been recently. We talked of needing physical affection in general, and I asked her if she had ever been curious about lesbian sex. Not hesitating a moment, she said that she had. Then she paused.

"I don't know if I should tell you this, but I have actually considered seducing you. With you knowing full well that it wouldn't mean anything more than friendship to me, of course, but to get that sexual gratification and physical closeness."

My heart leapt out of my shirt and in again, vacillating between my throat and my stomach. I could not believe I had just heard her say that.

"Why?" I managed to stammer out.

"Because I know that you would never hurt me, which would be very important, seeing as this would be my first time. And you could do amazing things to me. I have absolutely no doubt about that."

I didn't know what to do. For the first time in a long while, I was at a loss for words.

"Of course, you know that I could never start anything myself," she began slowly. "That would be taking initiative."

"But if I took initiative?" I asked.

"That's how it would have to happen," she said.

We started talking about what it would be like. She told me of her boundaries, like how she would not feel comfortable with any of her clothes off. The prospect sent shivers through me. She spoke of how she would want to do more than just kiss me, because that alone would not do much for her.

"However, I expect there are a lot of things that can be done beyond that while still keeping clothes on," she said.

I nodded slowly in agreement, eyes wide, still dumb-struck by the fact that this conversation was taking place.

We had planned to go to dinner earlier that evening, and at this point she asked me if I was hungry. My mouth was indeed watering, but logic told me that she must have meant for food. I told her yes. She said she thought it would be a good idea if we spent a little time apart before to "key down." Again, I agreed.

Neither one of us moved from our positions.

"What are we doing?" she asked.

"I don't know, what are we doing? Are we planning it?"

"Why else would we be talking about it this way?" she said.

We were both nervous as hell—she because of the new ground she was covering and I from the passion—and expressed this openly to each other. I wanted her so much I was shaking. I was even more nervous with the thought of her giving me her virginity. In the most personal terms, she was opening herself up to me in a way I had barely allowed myself to hope for. I couldn't remember a night I hadn't fallen asleep thinking about touching her, but I wasn't sure I was prepared for the responsibility of being her *first*. And why now, after all these months? I wondered if she was toying with me.

I looked at her, and it seemed as though her eyes pierced right into my soul. But instead of that intensity making me want to run away as it had in the past, the sheer arousal and intimate feelings it bred kept me anchored right where I sat. The tension hung so thick between us that I felt lost in it. I asked her if I could at least rub her shoulders, and she jumped about five feet.

"I wasn't prepared for this to happen so quickly," she said. "If I...and could you...God, I..."

"Jody, would you like me to do something?"

"Sydney, you know I could never say yes to that question."

The game was beginning.

"But could you say no?"

"I don't know what I would do if you did something to me right now."

I moved over to her. She was seated in my desk chair, and I knelt before her, staring into her gorgeous brown eyes. I took her left hand in mine and kissed it gently. She put her other hand up to her face and covered her eyes. In the moment, I thought she was concentrating on the sensations she was experiencing, but looking back I suspect the primary reason she didn't look at me was to make things easier. I kept my gaze upon her. I took each of her fingers into my mouth, caressing them with my tongue as my other hand stroked her thigh lightly. Her right hand came down and cupped my face, pulling me up to her. I kissed her neck, taking in her scent. She moved her face around to mine, and before I knew it we were kissing. It was slow at first, but she soon took the initiative and slipped her tongue into my mouth. My hands went to work; one fondling her magnificent breasts while the other was firmly fixed behind her neck, nestled in her long brown hair, keeping her close to me for fear that this was a dream. I closed my eyes and concentrated on remembering every moment.

Suddenly she laughed, pulled away from me, and apologized for being a poor kisser. "I have only kissed a few other people, and I am not well-versed in the matter."

"Don't worry about it. Relax," I said, my eyes gleaming with a combination of lust, love, and seductive cunning. Having gotten this far, there was no way I was going to let

Jody's performance anxiety get in the way of making love to her.

"Is this doing anything for you?" I asked between kisses.

"Well, I'm wearing really thick clothes." It was true. She had on a pair of blue jeans and a large university sweatshirt with just a bra underneath. I was wearing gray jeans and an ACLU T-shirt. I felt a tad helpless against the thick cotton of her clothing, but I continued nonetheless, hoping our kissing would spark something inside of her.

After about five minutes, she informed me that her chair was in the way, so I asked if she wanted to move to the bed. I got up, removed my shoes and hers, leapt onto my bed, and extended my hand for her to do the same. She chuckled, but then climbed onto the bed as well, and was soon lying next to me. I rolled on top of her, and we were instantly kissing again.

My mind was going absolutely crazy, replaying every fantasy that I had ever had about Jody. My hands roamed freely over her body, and her hands became fairly uninhibited as well. I had no idea she would be so passionate. For a moment I marveled at the seesaw of her emotions: from complete disinterest to smoldering desire. Eventually, her sweatshirt got pulled up a little, and my hand touched the bare skin of her stomach. I quickly pulled it away.

"What's wrong?"

"I just found a boundary."

"Oh. Well, I am discovering that my boundaries are moving a bit—under the shirt is all right."

I distinctly felt the pounding of my heart in other parts of my body, and I became slightly faint. My hands worked their way up the front of her chest, very slowly. I reached the base of her bra, and my fingertips traced the border all the way across her rib cage. My hand enveloped her breast, and I was overtaken with passion. I found her nipple and rolled it between my fingers through her bra. She responded with a little contented moan and promptly thrust her tongue deep into my mouth. Surprised at how much I had affected her, I continued with more intensity.

Then I realized that her hand had found its way up the right sleeve of my shirt and was stroking my shoulder extremely lightly. I have no idea how she knew this was an excellent way to turn me on, but she certainly had a knack for it. I was insane with desire. Things couldn't get much better.

"You know," she began, "I was just thinking about how this would be much easier if my shirt was off."

Stunned silence. Then: "Do you want to take off your shirt?"

"No. But you could take it off for me."

Yes, I could. Battling my lust, I stopped and looked into her eyes. "Are you sure?"

"Yes, Sydney. Yes. I want this." She ran her fingernails over my arms. "From you."

Doubt quickly quashed, my hands flew, succumbing to her calculated nonrequest. I pulled her to me so that she was sitting, making it easier for me to remove her shirt. I looked upon her naked stomach, and my eyes stopped on her breasts. Thinking better of it even as the words formed on my lips, I told her how beautiful they were. She seemed surprised, saying she had never thought they were that great. I told her I had been admiring them from afar for too long. She smiled, and pulled me down with her.

I decided to slow down a bit, as much as I could control, so I moved my hands and fingers with less vigor. I wanted this to last for a while. I rose up slightly, taking in the sensations: the contrast of my pale hand on her olive skin; the scent of her silky hair; the feel of her hands making their way up under my shirt, her fingertips and fingernails running lightly over my entire back. I was in heaven. She found my bra strap and asked me what my boundaries were.

"You can do anything you want," I said breathlessly.

"OK, then I won't ask anymore."

She unhooked my bra and continued to run her hands all over. Her fingers explored my breasts, alternating light and hard touches. I couldn't believe how she knew all of these things instinctively. She was the most acutely sensitive lover to ever touch me, and it reinforced my feeling that her reluctance to be with me had been born of fear and not lack of desire. She pinched a nipple between her fingers and gently rolled it around. I sucked my breath in sharply and stiffened. "I take it this is good?" she said mockingly.

"Everything you are doing is good," I replied and reassured her with a slow and deep kiss. I was holding nothing back; I was giving her all of me. I was fully clothed, but it was the most naked I had ever been.

I asked her what she was thinking, and between kisses, she started talking about a movie she'd been hired to do earlier in the year. Her role had required her to kiss Kellie on camera. Privately, I simply couldn't handle the thought of one of my friends kissing Jody, even if it was in the context of an acting job. Apparently, and completely unbeknownst to me, Jody had a hell of a time trying to keep me from seeing the film, and had avoided talking about it whenever possible. She knew how much it was hurting me, and she didn't want to cause me pain. I was taken aback by her words; despite her rejection of me as a romantic possibility, she'd been so sensitive to my feelings. As we kissed and touched each other, it became clear that her confession had led us into a different realm of sharing, one reserved for lovers, the kind that exists primarily in those intimate moments in bed. Another fantasy coming true.

"I can't believe I'm making love to you," I said. She smiled, and our mouths gently found each other again.

My hands traced the border between her bra and her skin, and she told me, "Sydney, you can take my bra off."

I struggled with the front-closing clasp; I couldn't get it undone.

"It's new, and a little hard to work with," she said laughing. "Let me help."

"No, I am going to do this," I said. When I finally got it open, she let out a slight sigh.

"Do you still like them?" she asked.

I moved my mouth forward in answer. My tongue traced little circles around her full breast, taking in the taste and texture of her skin. When I reached her nipple, I sucked and bit and pulled and licked. "Is any of this good?"

"Something you're doing is."

I tried it all again, and she let out a small moan when I pulled on her nipple with my teeth. I looked at her and commented on her cute little sounds.

"They're moans of contentment," she said. "This is so nice—I am so comfortable with you."

Her defenses had clearly lowered, and I was no longer convinced our play would end in a stalemate.

I caressed her breasts again with my mouth. I lifted my head to kiss her, and her fingers found my nipple. I suppressed a loud cry of ecstasy, not wanting to disturb the neighbors. "Jody, I am getting really excited. You may not want to do this, because if this continues, you may have to do something about it."

"You'll have to tell me what to do..."

But I was intent on this being her night for pleasure. Given that, I decided to be a bit more ambitious. I moved my hand between her legs, and received quite a nice reaction. I indulged myself and took the liberty of planting a kiss on her jeans. She shivered. My mouth found her lips again, and I started to rub her with strong and intense motions. I fingered the button on her jeans, but then stopped.

"I'll tell you if it's too far," she said breathlessly, as she grasped my shoulders. I watched the need for nonparticipation leave her face, easily replaced with the need for passion.

It took a bit of effort for me to unbutton her jeans. "They're a little hard to get off," she said. My next try worked. I slowly unzipped her pants and slid my hand into them. Her eyes were shut tight again, and this time I had no doubt that she was focused completely on my touch.

She was wearing a pad. I was a bit disappointed, but knew there were ways to work around it. I teased with light touches on the outside of her underwear, and then lifted my hand to go underneath. "Too far," Jody murmured and grabbed my wrist. I went back to rubbing little circles through the thick barrier of her undergarments. I let out a small laugh at the ridiculous nature of the situation, and she asked me if I was lost. I replied that I was, and that it was very difficult to do what I was doing through underwear and a pad.

"You're doing an amazing job," she gasped. My mind ran to fantasies of my tongue delving deeply inside of her, feeling the folds of her most intimate places and tasting her arousal. I could almost feel her clit against my lips as we kissed deeply and our tongues danced.

Suddenly Jody thrust her hips up into me, gripped the back of my neck, and dug her nails in slightly, leaving little scratches. I thought she'd just come, but she assured me it was just a rush of passion.

She continued to move her hands around my body. "It's strange; I don't mind being so exposed to you, but if you were half-naked, too, it would be uncomfortable. Are you always on top?"

"No," I answered. "I just thought it would be better if I were, at this point. Usually it's more fluid, depending on who is doing what."

"Not this time!" she said, and I laughed.

We continued talking and laughing and gasping and moaning. She dug her fingernails into the back of my neck twice more, and both times I felt her breathe into my ear a soft "Yes." Finally, she said that it had gone as far as it would, and that I could stop if I found a good point. I slowed down to just kissing and benign caressing, finally resting next to her and catching my breath. She let out a contented sigh, putting her arms around me. She said, "And this is never going to happen again."

Game over.

Or so I thought. For the next several months I continued to make love to her, at my request, which kept her securely in denial about her role. A year later she finally admitted we were lovers, but insisted that she wasn't in love. It was yet another game we would play indefinitely, a scrimmage with mismatched teams. The first time we finally made love to each other on equal emotional terms, a huge earthquake rocked Southern California. We always like to think we caused it.

Drag King Debutante

PEZ BOOTWALKER

I know this sounds weird, but there's this thing where if you have a Sam's Warehouse Club card you can get a Budget Rent a Car rental reservation through your card. That's what Alicia had done. She had gotten this car so that we could go to the drag king contest in Atlanta. It was me, Alicia, and Jake, who used to be Donna but now we called Jake. Alicia had a suitcase full of makeup, hair stuff, and costumes. Me and Jake already had some stuff to use: underwear, boots, and shoes.

"But you need a theme," Alicia had insisted days earlier when we decided to leave Jacksonville and enter the contest.

"That's right, a theme," Jake agreed. Jake had short, jet-black hair and was pretty built from working as a stock boi at (guess) Wal-Mart. I was the only one not connected to Sam Walton's empire somehow—well, except that I helped myself to a five-finger discount now and then. But not at the Walmart Jake worked at, because people knew we hung out and he'd get fired. Not the worst thing if you ask me, but you know.

"What about the time in high school we did 'N Sync at the talent show?" I asked.

"OK, now you're thinkin', but we didn't do drag, we just sang the song and danced. But, yeah, you're on track.

Cowboys, rednecks, gangsters, something."

"I've got it. Do vampires," Alicia said.

"Vampires don't sing," Jake said.

"I know, but it's original. OK, I've got it. Do a Moby song, start out like you're in one of those cool car commercials, then morph it into something."

"That's great," we agreed.

We were still rehearsing our songs and moving through the choreography in the car as Alicia drove to Atlanta. We sat in the back lot of Cheesy Chef drinking chemical-made malts and eating questionable fries near the Florida-Georgia border when a couple of assholes decided to yell shit at us. Alicia turned on the car and jammed it into gear in a split second then almost swerved into them, flinging her malt all over the biggest guy.

We screamed and yelled at them, but then thought, *Shit, Alicia, get us outta here.*

"They're nowhere near their truck, they can't catch us."

"You better be sure," Jake said.

"Fuck them," I said.

"Well, I guess I won't be able to mind the speed limit in Georgia." She made a face that said "yikes."

"That's not good." If you knew Georgia cops like we did, you'd be making faces, too.

We could have found some dykes to crash with, but we'd all been working and we wanted to treat ourselves right, so we got a Super 8 room in Atlanta and made the sink the wet bar. Filled it with ice, hung up our costumes, and lined our snacks up on the little wobbly round table that sat under bad floral curtains that reminded me of watching *Golden Girls* reruns with my aunt.

Alicia had brought bubble bath for the tub and some

candles. "Excuse me while I enjoy my own spa. I will just ignore the stickies on the bottom of the tub." She laughed and disappeared into the bathroom.

I had stolen a kid's sock from one of my little cousins, stuffed it with my mom's panty hose, and tied it off to make a softie. Jake saw it and started jumping around the room, making fun of me. "What's this?"

"It's a softie," I stated, and jerked it out of his hand, embarrassed for Alicia to see me with it. "It's a grower, not a shower. Ya know, until I meet the right gal, I don't wanna scare nobody."

"Aliciaaaaaa, Jamie's only gotta softieeeeee," Jake sang against the bathroom door.

"Shut up. And it's Pez. Don't forget."

"How can your head pop off if you don't even have a boner? Ha ha!" Jake fell onto the couch.

Getting into drag for the first time took about four hours. Of course we were drinking and goofing off as we went. I had to cut little hairs from the back of my head then use spirit gum to glue them to my face, making a little goatee and moustache. I wore a jock strap (five-finger discount from Sears) and stuffed my little bulge into place before pulling on some secondhand men's suit pants.

"Can you even see it?" I asked.

Alicia rubbed her butt against me and said, "Maybe I can feel it." And giggled. I suddenly didn't just think of her as Alicia from my street. I got confused.

"Do you want help with your chest?" she asked.

"Huh? Yeah. Here, Jake, can you? No, no, I got it. Never mind." I turned away from both of them and concentrated on the mirror. I held an Ace bandage up with my thumb and tried to wrap it around with one hand but kept screwing it up.

"Just let me help," Alicia said. She grabbed the tangled brown elastic. "Here, hold here, and turn when I tell you." She wrapped me up and secured it with those little metal-toothed clips. Then she smiled at me in that friendly way she always does. We're just friends. Superclose great friends, right?

"Now I'm getting ready...alone," she announced and locked herself into the bathroom. She emerged through the door backward, her ass looking great in a pair of skintight, leopard stretch pants, then she slowly turned to face us to reveal a bustier, old-fashioned hair rollers, bright-blue eye shadow, and a full face of makeup—and then we saw the real shockers! She had made a mustache for herself, too, and had a dildo in her pants. "I'm a not-finished drag queen! I had to run off to the ball before I could shave or tuck!"

Jake laughed and laughed and fell to the floor, holding his gut and crossing his legs so he wouldn't pee. I stood in shock till I finally laughed, too—largely because Jake was so funny laughing and hiccuping.

We got in the car and made it to the club alive since Jake drove—Jake only smoked pot and didn't drink.

The club was over 18 for the night so we didn't need our fake IDs, just a flask of Malibu Rum to spike our Coke. My body loosened and my eyes soaked up all the cool drag kings and their fags or babes. I took a few mental notes for the future. I got a surge in my jock when I got cruised a few times. Jake didn't take long to find a babe and a corner to make out in. I had to grab him by the collar when the contest started. We did the gig and pretty girls screamed at us from the front of the stage. I counted in my head to remember my steps, but I took a moment here and there to wink or do an "I'm checkin' you out" point and smile at the gals.

When Alicia crawled out of our cardboard car, the audience howled with laughter and she exaggeratedly grabbed her crotch like an embarrassed drag queen. We were pretty drunk by then, too—or maybe it was just my first screaming crowd—but it all went into a haze in my mind. I heard later that I did my steps and lip syncing right, but I don't even remember. I know my face hurt from smiling the next day. I think I cracked my spirit gum, too.

I stumbled off the stage and immediately this hot chick with pink hair and a swishing chest was in my arms. We started kissing against the wall. I had a moment wondering where my crew was, but I got lost in her mouth.

Suddenly I felt nails scrape firmly down my neck, I pulled back my head with a "Yowww." Alicia's freaky face appeared over my shoulder and her bulge pressed into my ass. "Honey, aren't you going to introduce me to your friend?"

"I, I...Alicia, you're drunk. I lost you. Don't they want us onstage?"

"I think we're all wanted in the bathroom." The pink-haired girl grabbed my hand as I followed Allie into the bathroom and a black-painted stall. "You're here." She slammed the new chick against the stall wall. "You're here." She put me facing the girl. "And I'm back here." Pinky wrapped her hand around my head and we started kissing again. She had on a little rocker girl tank top with WORSHIP ME on it, and her chest pushed up soft under my hands. Her mouth tasted like bubble gum, whiskey, and cigarettes.

Hands seemed to be everywhere. Someone undid my belt buckle, then a pair of hands went down my pants, squeezing my ass. At one point I went to squeeze Pinky's tits but there was already a hand there.

I started grinding back into the finger working around my asshole. And a voice growled into my ear, "You little faggot. You thought you could get some pussy and you would forget about your man hole, but you can't get rid of your faggot nature that easy. You know you just want a big daddy cock up there."

I had my hand up Pinky's skirt and wasn't thinking about safe sex or clean fingers, I am embarrassed to report. She grabbed my hand and said, "Hey, Mr. Boi, some Jack will sanitize these," and pulled the cherry from her drink, popped that into her mouth, poured her straight whiskey drink over my hand, then shoved it back into her warm self. Her pussy felt so warm and wonderful. She was very wet. I slid one finger in between her slick lips and inside her.

Behind me, one hand was grabbing and working my ass-meat while the other was working my boi-hole. I soon felt a hard and smooth coolness near my hole, and the sound of spit flying.

"Oh, God" was all I could mutter. I'm surprised I didn't have the spins. But I did almost lose my balance. I took a deep breath and focused on the tits in front of me again and on the job my hand had to do. Pinky was climbing a high and moaning and writhing on my finger. "More, c'mon." I put two more fingers in her and got a good rhythm going. My own pussy was getting juicy from the action behind it.

Alicia dug her teeth into my neck like a stud cat holding down its mate, then she pushed the head against my ass more fervently. "Do you think you can take it, faggot?"

I pulled my head back from Pinky, moaned yes, and pushed my ass back onto Alicia's cock.

My hole strained just a split second then swallowed the head of her cock. She slowly eased it in, then pulled back just a bit to deliver more spit. She reached around and smashed her hand around mine in Pinky's cunt, saying "I need some juice to lube you up." She sort of half finger-fucked Pinky along with me, our fingers together for a moment, then she pulled hers away. Next I felt a warm slickness on her dick that made it even better in my ass. Alicia could tell, from my grinding hips and moans, that she could really start fucking me. I had dreamed of a cock in my ass but never knew how that could happen since I liked girls so much. Remember, I was 18, and even though I thought I was so cool I hadn't done or read all that much. (Still working on it, as a matter of fact.)

As she fucked me harder, I fucked Pinky harder. Two rhythms were confusing, so I lodged my elbow against my stomach and made my arm a stiff ramming cock. Pinky pulled her arms out of her shirt and held the top of the stall wall. I sucked and bit at her nipples like my life depended on it. I just wanted her to come because I could tell I was near and wouldn't be able to concentrate much longer. My ass sucked and kissed at Alicia's cock. My pants hung around my ankles, and Alicia delivered smacks to my ass cheek as she fucked me. Pinky squealed, "Yes, yes, oh, yes, just keep fucking me!" then jerked and convulsed into wave after wave of orgasm. She bent forward, squishing my face into her chest. I reached past her with both hands and held the wall. I didn't care if I *was* smashing her. I knew I could have an ass orgasm if I just had someone to grind against. Pinky lifted her thigh into me and Alicia fucked smooth and hard, growling into my ear, "Come for your Queen Daddy," and bit into my neck again. I shuddered with a burning all over that I can't explain. I know it was an ass come. My legs jerked and my breath came in shakes. Just then, and I know it sounds weird but it's true (maybe he'd been waiting for a calm moment this whole time, I don't know), Jake *pounded* on the stall door, scaring the tar out of all three of us. "C'mon, Pez, we gotta get near the stage. You missed the other acts."

"Comin'!" I yelled.

"I should say so," Alicia mumbled.

As we were opening the door, Jake was saying, "Have you seen Alish-aaaah?" And when he saw her he said, "I don't wanna know," and he laughed.

I felt all wonderful and jelly-bodied, but when I looked at Alicia I almost got scared. I think the pink-haired girl might have been scared, too, at least when her whiskey wore off the next morning, because I gave her my E-mail but she never wrote.

I tried to kiss Alicia later only to learn that spirit gum stinks and I don't know how the girls do it (kiss us kings, that is). We waited to play more until the makeup and bits of hair were gone. Oh, and we came in third, by the way. I think the crowd appreciated our effort.

Choosing

LYDIA SWARTZ

By the time it was my turn to share, I was fighting tears and sleepiness.

My lover, T.J., had dragged me to yet another meeting. This time it was PFLAG on a muggy September evening. The heat pressed me into the pungent cushions of the ancient sofa in the church basement. For an hour, I had listened as queer sons and daughters and parents of queers told their stories. It was 1989, deep in the AIDS era, and there was so much unfinished business in this room. My eyes were puffy with tears.

I didn't have anything to say to these hurting people. I had hoped time would run out before it was my turn to speak. But it hadn't.

I was brief. I said, "I choose."

Major General (Ret.) Brassball, a huge man with a crew-cut whose estranged son had come out to him two weeks before the boy died, stopped writing. The major had been covering page after page of his steno notebook as everybody talked, sometimes interrupting a speaker to ask for clarification. But in the silence after my two words, not even the major's pen moved.

I went on.

"I am technically bisexual, but I love women. I prefer

women. I choose to make my life with a woman and within the lesbian community."

This was not one of those meetings where cross talk is discouraged. In fact, I had observed that this was a setting where every speaker got feedback. Laughter and hugs were normal responses. People blurted out advice and their own stories. But the room was quiet after I spoke. Everybody found something besides me to look at. I waited. Dust motes danced in the splash of light from a torchère in the corner.

"I'm done," I said, finally.

The young woman next to me immediately launched into a story about trying to find a token boyfriend in junior high after she figured out why the other girls on her lacrosse team wouldn't shower when she was in the locker room. Major General Brassball's pen got busy again. Men and women nodded and laughed.

I looked across the room to where T.J. was sitting. She avoided my eyes.

At the post-meeting tea-and-cookies hour, I picked up a PFLAG brochure. I had plenty of time to read it, because nobody wanted to talk to me. The brochure reassured parents of queers that it was *not their fault*. Their sons and daughters *could not help it*. Queerness was inborn, probably a random chemical aberration *in utero*. Nobody, after all, would *choose such a difficult life*.

I had heard these things before. I'd also been informed, authoritatively, that I wasn't really bisexual; I was only clinging to that identification because I wasn't brave enough to embrace the label "lesbian." I had flirted with many lesbians who found me suddenly uninteresting when I said the "b" word, even if I pointed out that she, the lesbian, had been with more men than I had, and more recently. I could have been a lot more popular if I'd just kept my mouth shut.

Despite all this, I did have a girlfriend—a butch, political, sexually conservative girlfriend, in fact. Somehow it worked. I allowed T.J. to drag me to meetings. T.J. allowed me to have my sexual adventures as long as I came right home and told her all about it and we could stay up the rest of the night fucking. We were happy.

It was during one of my extracurricular adventures that I met Minnie.

The first time I saw her, she was working the door at some sort of tantric women's orgy. Minnie had neatly trimmed dark hair—by a No. 2 clipper, I assessed. Her eyes shone light and curious, and were the kind that changed color from green to blue to hazel depending on her mood and the light. She dressed in that crisp, simple, baby dyke fat girl style, all dark colored cotton fading at the seams.

Minnie returned my admiring gaze and let a grin take over her face.

I wanted her, but I knew she was way too young and too butch for me. I opened the door to the party room and sighed. Soon, probably within the next hour, somebody would tell Minnie the truth about me. I basked in the memory of her grin and felt certain it was the last one I'd get from her.

The next time I saw Minnie we were in the sweet, swampy dregs of that night.

The orgy organizers knew what they were doing. They led us in visualizations and tantric breathing, then when the entire room rumbled with sexuality, they turned us loose on one another. I had spent what seemed like days between the parallel temple columns of a pair of bicycle-muscled thighs, worshiping a gushing fount of amrita. A dakini behind me slowly, and with tender relentlessness, fucked me with an uncompromisingly hard dildo, then her hand.

When I noticed Minnie across the room, my threesome had collapsed into a panting, moist, not very tantric pile. Minnie sat cross-legged, naked, and beaming at me across a choppy sea of male and female bodies. My cunt, which should have been sated by then, flip-flopped. I turned back to my threesome so we could exchange introductions.

I didn't talk to Minnie that night. By the time everybody was pulling on clothes and hugging, she was gone. But I made sure to find out who she was before I left.

T.J. stirred and moaned when I slid my freshly showered body between the covers and spooned her. I began to tell T.J. about what I'd done and what I'd felt. She didn't wake up, but she wasn't exactly asleep either. I knew she heard me.

As I murmured into her neck, I reached around and slid my fingers between T.J.'s legs, stroking her as I supplied detail after detail. She rocked her hips back into my belly and forward into my hand, moaning and grinding on my fingers when I got to the good parts. My lover's pleasure set me off again.

I admit I closed my eyes a few times and thought about Minnie in my arms—even though I knew that butch baby dyke wouldn't let me touch her once she found out I was bisexual. And when I finally fell asleep at dawn, Minnie did play a part in my dreams.

I got busy with work after that. T.J. went out of town on political business. Since we had an agreement that I would only have adventures when I could come home, crawl in bed with her, and spill the whole tale, I spent my nights with my vibrator.

Months passed before I next ran into Minnie. T.J. was home by then and I was at another woo-woo women's sex event.

Candles warmed the room, and I had brought my favorite cinnamon spice massage oil. Carrying the bottle had already scented my fingers. The afternoon sun filtered through the white sheets that covered the windows, giving everyone a soft Hollywood glow. Somebody guided an opening circle then we followed instructions to arrange ourselves around three massage tables. Of the eight women there, six were familiar. I'd shared tables with them before—Minnie was new.

I'd immediately noticed Minnie's presence, of course. She wore a T-shirt short enough for her nice round belly to peek out above her sweatpants. I knew we'd both be naked soon, but that peek of belly—even more than her naked, voluptuous body—did me in. I felt hot. I felt tongue-tied. I felt like I was at a high-school dance instead of at a women's sensual massage exchange.

I hung back, fingering my bottle of oil. I tried not to stare at Minnie. I tried not to let the other women catch my eye.

When I finally looked up, Minnie was standing in front of me, grinning that irresistible grin.

"Looks like it's you and me," she said.

I hadn't heard Minnie's voice before. It was big, like her, wholesome and enthusiastic, like a gym teacher explaining the rules of the game. I dropped the oil, and when I bent down to pick it up, so did she—and we bonked heads. We laughed and touched each other's head. The oil bottle rolled away until it lodged under the closest massage table.

Minnie got down on her hands and knees. She reached under the table, leaving her sweet round ass sticking up. I took some deep breaths. *Mustn't slap. Mustn't touch yet.*

She stood up, then we made our way toward the one open table, our table.

Once we had both disrobed, we stood next to the sheet-draped massage table and shyly ogled each other. We could hear the quiet conversations of the women at the other tables. Hands slid on flesh. Women sighed and sank into pleasure around us. The air in the room was thick with hot wax, warm oil, and girl scent.

"I'm bi, you know," I exclaimed.

The silence stretched forever. I counted 10 heartbeats.

"Oh," Minnie said. "OK."

We both examined the sheet on the table for a while.

"Do you want to go first, or should I?" she said.

"You go," I said.

Minnie crawled up onto the massage table, settled herself facedown, and laid her hands at her sides, palms up.

"What would you like?" I asked. "Anything need work? Anything I should stay away from?"

"No oil in my hair or on my face," came Minnie's muffled voice. "Other than that, go for it."

"Really?" I asked, a little more breathlessly than I had planned.

"Really!" she replied.

A butch baby dyke who trusts a bi woman to work the controls?

I felt honored. I felt humbled. I felt intimidated. I was eager to go for it.

I opened the bottle of oil and tipped it over Minnie's back, between her shoulder blades. I drizzled a line of oil down her spine and then across her butt cheeks, then began spreading the oil across the broad mounds and valleys of her back and ass.

Minnie is new, I thought. *Does Minnie know what we do here?*

I kneaded the muscles in her shoulders near her spine. Minnie groaned very quietly, in a high, little-girl voice. I put the palms of my hands on her shoulder blades, pressed in hard, and rotated them.

Does she have a girlfriend? Does she know I have a girl-friend?

I ran my fists down either side of her spine, then pressed them into the indentations at the base of her spine, just above where her ass rose magnificently from her waist. Minnie grunted. Her ass lifted into the pressure. Her hands curled into soft fists.

Is she vanilla? Will she tense up if I touch her asshole?

I lightly slapped her butt cheeks with the backs of my hands, alternating slaps with very slow scratches, digging in my close-cropped fingernails and raking them through the meat of her ass. I flattened my hands on her cheeks and slid them apart, exposing her butt hole, then together. Minnie's arms spread and she gripped the sides of the table. Her legs spread apart and her toes dug into the sheet-draped surface of the massage table.

"I'm coming up, OK?" I said.

Minnie exhaled a "Yesssssss" as I vaulted onto the table and kneeled between her legs.

I used the advantage of my new position to put some hard pressure on Minnie's back. I placed my elbows on her waist and ran them up either side of her spine.

"Ohhh," Minnie groaned.

I pushed myself up, then leaned in hard, working first the left side of her back then the right side with my palms and knuckles. My knees pressed into the sweet darkness between her legs—her thick, wet fur. Was she arching her back? Was she pressing her vulva against my knees? Yes. Probably. No, definitely, she definitely was.

Is this really an invitation, or just a spinal reflex? Will she resent me for taking advantage of her physical vulnerability?

I leaned forward and lay on top of her, my breasts pressing into her back. I knew she could feel my own wetness against her ass. I put my elbows next to her ears and I grabbed knucklefuls of hair at the back of her head. She gasped. Her head rose slightly, even though I wasn't pulling enough of her hair to move her.

I rocked my hips against her ass. When she pushed against me, I rewarded her with harder thrusts. She did not fight me. She did not go still and shy. She fucked me back. The massage table squeaked with our combined weight. It would either hold or not hold. I didn't care.

"Roll over," I growled into her ear, then I got up on my hands and knees and moved back on the table to give her some room.

It was a narrow massage table and Minnie was a big, healthy girl. But even allowing for all that, she took more than her fair share of time rolling over. She looked at me to make sure I was watching. She let me admire her thighs, her ass, her belly, her breasts. She spread herself out before me, finally, somehow managing to stare at me boldly and shyly at the same time. *Here I am,* she seemed to say. *What are you going to do about it?*

That was a good question, given I had less than half an hour before the timekeeper hit the chime indicating "switch."

And given that I didn't know Minnie at all, I had to

guess. Was she the kind of butch with a soft creamy center? Or the kind who would be infuriated by tenderness? Minnie was young. She seemed aggressive. My guess was she'd come out as a toddler and had been barking orders at femmes since she was 10. I must be her first bi-girl. For her, this was probably an adventure in letting go. I chose door number two.

Next to each table, the event coordinators had arranged a TV tray with latex gloves, a moist towel, lubes and oils, dry towels, and cornstarch. I reached over and to clean the oil off my hands with the moist towel, then wiped them on a dry towel. I pulled on a pair of latex gloves. I grabbed the water-based lube.

I looked down at Minnie. She was staring at me seriously. No smile. She did not look critical or apprehensive, just interested. Her eyes had gone deep green and a little watery.

I bent over her, brushing her with my breasts. I cupped her left breast and took her nipple into my mouth. My tongue played with it. I rested the fingers of my other hand between her cunt lips, barely moving. As I sucked and tweaked her nipple, her cunt heated. Soon, she was soaking wet. Her hips vibrated, eager for my fingers.

Not so fast. You're going to find out what a bi-girl is capable of, Miss Boy.

Slowly and powerfully, I nipped and sucked her nipple. At the same time, I let my fingers rock and slide through her eager slit, long strokes, hard but not hard enough, and not nearly as fast as she wanted. With each stroke, I paused just long enough over her clit to make her pelvis strike at me, trying to get that hook in its greedy mouth.

My own cunt dripped and throbbed, demanding that I proceed with dispatch. *No!* I replied. My clit responded with an almost-painful jolt of need. I sped up.

I let go of Minnie's tit and crouched entirely between her thighs, which were frog-legging, jerking, trying to suck me into the wet red need at her center.

Oh, God, she was beautiful. She reeked of girl. Her fur was shiny with her own juices. Her inner and outer labia were swollen, the inner labia pushing the outer aside.

Because I wore gloves, I squirted a big glob of lube onto the top of Minnie's moist slit. I didn't want to hurt her—not that way.

I bent down and put my face as close as I could get to Minnie's twat without actually touching it. Her girl smell overwhelmed the lube. My tongue wanted to touch her, but I was good. (T.J. and I had strict fluid agreements.) Instead, I grabbed a handful of pubic hair in each fist and pulled apart Minnie's cunt lips. I exhaled hot air on the hooded goddess inside.

Minnie writhed and whimpered. So close. So needy. Such sweet begging. Minnie didn't need words; her ass was communicating loud and clear.

Aware of the clock and stabbed by my own impatient cunt, I didn't make Minnie wait any longer. I found her hard clit under its thick hood—if I was Minnie's girlfriend, I'd get a ring in that thing right away—and I pressed it. I pressed it with three fingers, then started circling, paying careful attention to what different directions did to her, how she reacted to 2 o'clock versus 7 o'clock.

My other hand found Minnie's eager cunt hole, which was already pulsed and grabbed like a barnacle underwater. I slid one finger inside slowly. She hollowed around it, then clamped down. *One finger not enough!* her cunt screamed.

Two fingers, three fingers, and her cunt wanted more.

But not yet. She wouldn't get it yet. Instead, I curled those three fingers around and pressed my fingertips to the spot behind her clit, to the root of it, the ON button inside.

Her clit and her ass and her gasps taught my fingers exactly what tune to play. I went from *mezzoforte* to *fortissimo* and from *allegretto* to *vivace*. Minnie's ass rewarded me with rolling thrusts, and she went from gasping to hooting. I kept my fingers on her G spot, regardless of the wild ride that wrenched my wrist. Oh, and I was hooting now, too.

Even in a completely silent world, I would have known what was happening, because I was inside Minnie. Her vagina gathered itself, opening like the ocean sucking water off sand before the big wave strikes. Her preorgasmic contractions squeezed my fingers. Minnie blared orgasmic energy, which traveled up my arm and through my spinal cord. When her cunt clamped down on my hand in big waves, I rolled with the power, too.

I didn't have to think too much about what I was doing. My hand knew to pull back between waves. My fingertips knew to press together and slide sideways. As the wave crested, Minnie's cunt swallowed my whole hand as though it belonged deep inside her.

I did belong deep inside Minnie.

Minnie babbled. She sounded like the sound tracks of a dozen porn films remixed by King Tubby.

I curled my hand inside Minnie, palm up in a fist, knuckles against her G spot, and I pulled gently toward me, pressing the root of her pleasure, the source of her clit. She squeezed me hard. She said *No no no no no*, which meant *Yes yes yes yes yes*. I kept my thumb on her clit and moved my own hips in rhythm with the waves in her. I pushed all the red energy from my root into her. I shoved my red-hot energy cock into her.

Take that, baby butch, take it from the bi-girl.

Minnie was crying now, or laughing.

I left my hand inside her, cramped and burning, and I slid up her sweaty body to kiss her jaw, starting from her right ear and working my way slowly up to her left ear. She gradually settled down, taking deep full breaths, catching one on a little post-orgasmic sob. She wore a permanent, helplessly goofy grin.

Take that!

"Oh," she said, then stopped. Her mouth worked. She was going to try for a sentence. "I think I'm," she said. "It is."

I slid back down her body, sat up between her legs. Her hips bunched and her cunt squeezed, and she grunted as she shot my hand out of her—along with a cute little fart.

"Oh!" she said, looking confused. "I didn't know."

"It's all right," I said. I chuckled. "It's all good..." and then I was drowned out by a chime as loud as the inside of a bell steeple at noon.

"Time for the next person to get on the table," some cheery bitch called out from across the room. "Time to switch. Take a 10-minute break to change sheets and drink some water or take a pee break, if you need it."

Our break went on a little longer. No one seemed inclined to come over to our table, where I idly stroked Minnie, waiting for her to become capable of sitting up, then standing, then toddling to the bathroom.

When Minnie got back from the bathroom, I had rearranged the lube, oil, and linens on the TV tray. I sat cross-legged on a fresh, dry sheet on the massage table.

"Um, hi," she said. The dear baby dyke blushed. She actually blushed. "What would you like?"

I lay back and arranged myself on the table. I looked up at her coyly.

"You know what to do," I said. "You just be your butch little baby dyke self and I'll cope."

"Um..." she said, blushing deep red now. She looked at my kneecaps and rubbed the edge of the sheet with her fingers. "Um..."

"It's OK. I think I understand. Your girlfriend doesn't want you to do something like that to me, right?" I said gently.

"Oh, it's not that," she said.

Here it comes. Here's the part where she talks about her boundaries with bisexuals. I sighed and waited.

"It's just that I've never been with a woman before. I'm not sure how to please you, and I would really like to, especially after...after, well, you know..."

"You have, you never, you...*what*?"

"My husband and I are trying to get pregnant," she said so quietly I could barely hear her. "He asked me not to let other men fuck me while we're trying to get pregnant, so I started coming to these, and anyway, I've always wondered about girls, and..."

"Husband?" I bleated.

"Don't you have a boyfriend, too? Somebody told me you and your partner had an agreement..."

"Boyfriend?"

"Yeah, they told me..."

I wish I could have stopped laughing, but it was not in my power. Poor Minnie looked crestfallen.

Eventually I did stop laughing, of course, and I still had time to give Minnie a 20-minute lesson in how to do girls.

The Light at the End of the Road

KARLA HODGE

At the end of my parents' road lived Miss Williams. She didn't have kids of her own, but when her sister died of ovarian cancer Miss Williams took in her niece, Julie, and raised her. Other than Julie occasionally baby-sitting me, or the swap of a recipe now and then, we didn't really socialize with them. Julie grew up and left home. Miss Williams never married or seemed interested in men. My aunt said that was because she'd seen that getting knocked up by a man had killed her sister. For some reason, I bought that explanation for years.

After I left for college, I never thought much about Miss Williams or anyone back home, except when Mom ran down her usual list of gossip to tell me who'd died or who'd "run off" with whom (a recent fascination with divorces caused by Internet romance) or who'd had a tumor or body part removed. Pretty morbid.

"Well, not everybody has their head in some dirt, Karla," Mom would say when I protested this type of news. I've always had "my head in some dirt." I love gardening, working the soil, seeing what I can help blossom, what worked in our Ohio climate and what didn't. I began university to study agriculture, which meant I didn't get to touch the earth as much as I wanted.

After my sophomore year I debated whether to stay at school for the summer. Mom insisted I could get work at home helping Gyles Hall with his construction company—he would recommend me to his customers for landscaping. That sounded like a perfect deal and a good way to build up some references and experience.

Sweat trickled down my temples as I loaded some fertilizer into the back of my pickup truck at our local farm and tractor supply store. I had paused with my hand on my hip when I heard, "Karla? Karla Hodge? Why, you have grown up into a strong, hearty woman."

"Oh, hey there, Miss Williams." I hadn't seen her in a while.

"How have you been?"

"I'm fine. Fine. I'm working for old man Hall's construction company. He's tippin' me off to some landscaping jobs. How are you?" I took in her T-shirt and khakis. She didn't seem to have aged much. Her reddish brown hair was pushed behind her ears, but a few rebel curls hung around her face.

"I started to say, didn't think your Mom and Dad needed this much fertilizer. I gotta tell you, I always knew you were gonna be independent. In high school you started the strike for free speech at the school newspaper."

"Really? It's funny that you remember that." I wiped the sweat from my forehead and took off my working gloves.

"Oh, yeah, I remember. And now running your own landscaping."

"Why, I wouldn't say it's my own business just yet. I gotta go back to school in the fall."

"Oh, of course. But it sure is a start. Listen, I know how it is around the folks: If you need to just get out and have a

cup of tea or a soda don't stop yourself from comin' by."
She pulled a baseball cap onto her head and patted me on
the shoulder. We said polite goodbyes and I headed off with
my supplies.

One night while sitting on my parents' back patio I realized I couldn't stomach listening to one more detailed
analysis of my cousin's decision to elope and what it meant
to my aunt and blah, blah, blah. I remembered Miss
Williams's offer, told the folks I was "headin' out," and
walked down to her place.

She answered the door wearing cutoffs and a powder-
blue tank top that showed off her fit body. I caught myself
staring at her chest. I guess I felt she should be dressing like
my mom. But when I thought about it, I realized my mom
did wear cutoffs to mow the lawn. She just didn't look as
good. I couldn't believe I was thinking this stuff. Even
though I was 20, I hadn't been in bed with a man or a
woman. I thought something was wrong with me because I
really just preferred working with flowers and plants to
dealing with people. The thing with the high school newspaper was a fluke. It all started because I was "agriculture
editor" and had wanted to run a painting by Georgia
O'Keefe. Someone on the school board charged obscenity
and demanded my public apology. Kim Hicks, paper editor,
is actually the one who publicized the episode. My stance
seemed simple: There was nothing wrong with running the
picture, and I would not apologize. That was the most
attention I'd ever gotten and I don't know that I liked it.

Back to my social life: I didn't have one. And regarding
sex...I don't know. I guess I thought it was just something
popular girls talked about. I'd had a few crushes on some

girls in high school and this one chick in my English class, but nothing that overwhelmed me. Miss Williams, though, was beginning to overwhelm me.

"Well, hi there. Glad you came over. Want some iced tea or a soda?" She motioned me in. She had pictures of her family around and some old movie posters framed. No JCPenney showroom special. Her home breathed with real furniture. "I hope you don't mind that I have the AC off. I'm trying to keep these bills down, and tonight seemed bearable without it."

"Oh, that's fine, Miss Williams. I like it. Working out in the heat then coming into the air conditioning isn't too good for me anyway."

"Stop calling me Miss Williams. It sounds like a substitute teacher. My name is Evelyn."

We sat outside in her swing and talked about all kinds of things. We laughed a lot together. I really liked her. I didn't know how to deal with this new crush coming on. It seemed more intense than all the others.

For the next few weeks of summer I hung out at her house as much as possible. Subconsciously, I tried to protect us from gossip by working on her yard. Not that we needed protecting. We hadn't done anything yet. But why would two women 20 years apart in age be hanging out so much?

I looked up at Craig, who was waiting on me and my cousin Jenny at Zippy Spaghetti. Craig sat the warm basket of breadsticks in front of me and announced, "Everybody says you've got something going on with that old maid at the end of your road."

I dropped my fork and my chin.

Jenny gasped. "Did ya have to say it like that, Craig? Jeez."

I looked at her incredulously. "What? First of all, she's not *old*. Secondly, I am doing *yard work* for her. I'm working for Old Man Hall too. Do ya think I'm sleeping with him?"

"Hey, I'm just reporting the weather, not making it. Here's your garlic butter." He walked away.

I didn't want to tell Evelyn. What if she wouldn't let me come over anymore? But I also didn't want her hearing it from someone else. The next time I visited her, I attempted a subtle approach while we were in the kitchen. "You know, it seems Mom is always gossiping about somebody."

"She likes to stay informed, huh?" Evelyn didn't look up from the dishes she was scrubbing.

"Yeah. *You*...don't take notice of that stuff too much, do you?" I leaned against the counter, sipping my tea and looking over the glass at her face.

Evelyn stopped washing and wiped her hands on a dishtowel. "Karla, there's an old saying that I put my own twist on. If you're gonna do the time then you might as well do the crime. Make sense to you?"

She bent forward and, with her soft mouth, she kissed me. I never knew what a kiss could feel like. I had barely tried it before her and now my entire body felt like it could explode. Our mouths pressed softly together then harder as our passion deepened. We kissed and kissed, sucking and nibbling and tasting skin and lips and mouth. I moaned. I thought my legs would collapse. She leaned into me, breathing heavily, wrapping her arms around me and sliding her strong hands up my spine.

"Oh, Evelyn" was all I could manage as we fell to the

floor. I bit her neck, feeling her downy hair on my lips, feeling the tension of her muscles.

She pulled my shirt over my head and took my nipple into her mouth. My fingers splayed out as I tensed on her linoleum, and I gasped loudly. I never knew anything could feel that good. Her hair tantalized me. I pushed my hands into her curls and stroked her face as she kissed down my belly. "No, wait," I breathed.

She looked up. "What? Don't you want this?" She brought her mouth up to mine again, and we kissed for a long time. Her mouth tasted sweet like the strawberries I loved to grow. I suddenly knew the meaning of every love song. For the first time ever, I understood that I was a sexual creature.

"I want to try, um…" I paused, blushing. "Sixty-nining? Is that what it's called? Where we do stuff to each other at the same time?"

Evelyn smiled at me. For a brief second her eyes conveyed my innocence. "Yes, yes. I'll show you. Let's go to my bed." She rapidly unbuttoned her shirt and kicked off her shorts.

"No, stay." I didn't think I could walk and was afraid somehow everything would be messed up if we even stopped for a minute. Her small breasts hung down. My head swayed. I only wanted to grab her and consume her and touch her everywhere. She pulled off my clothes as we continued to kiss, then I lay back and she turned around so she straddled my face.

Her pussy smelled wonderful. I pressed my face against the soft skin of her thigh. *Women are so soft and beautiful,* I thought. *Evelyn is so soft and beautiful.* She was pure beauty—even though she was raw and real and tough. She wasn't artificial beauty like a pageant queen or a magazine centerfold. She smelled like a flower, and her palms were rough. "Gentle at first," she said, then lowered her pussy onto my mouth. At the same time I felt wet heat against mine. I gasped loudly, almost a scream. Her mouth worked such magic on me that I couldn't concentrate. I tried to aim each of my gasps and clenches forward so that my mouth at least landed on her. She laughed, telling me not to worry about it, to just relax and enjoy myself. Her nose smashed into my vagina and toward my asshole as her tongue lapped at my clitoris. I spread my legs as far as I could and took in the visual of her gorgeous, pink pussy—I could see and smell her beautiful asshole. So that's what they were really like! Evelyn made me gyrate with lust. I held her thighs and massaged her ass as she sucked and licked and stroked my cunt with her tongue. I wanted her to bury her entire face between my thighs.

When I really started to moan, she smashed her pink pussy into my mouth and I devoured her. She tasted fantastic. Her clit and lips slicked over my chin and back again for more, and I lapped wider and longer like a dog. I was a nasty doggy, a pure slut, an out-of-control bad girl. I licked and I sucked, transporting what she did to me with her mouth back into her own cunt. We rocked and rose on the same high until I started coming. I screamed into her pussy, which made her come, too, and she pounded her clit against my teeth. My body clenched and jerked in wave after wave.

Finally, we were able to take some deep and relaxing breaths. Evelyn clumsily turned around and collapsed in the crook of my arm. I kissed her sweaty and juicy face, pushing loose tendrils of hair from her forehead.

We fell into a love-induced sleep on the kitchen floor,

then moved ourselves to her bed. She pushed her finger into me, and I thought I would die and go to heaven right that second. How could one little finger feel so good? I kept saying, "What are you doing down there?" She laughed at how blown away I was. She started calling me "Bloomer," short for "late bloomer"—not that 20 is late for intercourse, but I was late on *everything*. I hadn't even a clue. If I had, I'm sure I would have gotten my head out of the dirt a lot sooner. Evelyn sat between my legs, her breasts jiggling with every slow stroke into me, then she pumped my pussy faster with her strong, rough hands until I went wild, halfway sitting up and jerking myself on her as we stared into each other's eyes. We fucked, we slept, we fucked some more. I made her teach me how to curl my fingers up into her special spot. I wanted to make her moan and writhe like she'd done to me. I loved the freckles on her chest. I loved her. I loved every inch of her—and her mind and spirit, too.

If it wasn't for her maturity I would have totally blown off my job—references be damned. I wanted to stay in bed with her forever. The town gossiped a lot that summer. But Mom couldn't even fathom that I was a dyke, so she just brushed off my time with Miss Williams as a purely gardening relationship.

Learning by Example

RACHEL KRAMER BUSSEL

Sheila dragged me over to the office kitchen during our coffee break, eager to confide something. She made me stand right next to her so she could whisper as quietly as possible.

"Did you see last night's episode?"

I knew, of course, that she was talking about *Office Scandal,* our favorite television show, which followed single women who worked together and who usually wound up in some compromising positions that were always the talk of the entire office, if not the entire city of New York. Last night's episode had been the much-talked-about event where Donna and Carla have an extended make-out session and some sizzling (and unexpected) sexual tension. Sheila knew I, being a lesbian, would be sure to appreciate it. I wasn't so sure what her reaction would be or why she was whispering in the kitchen. "Yes, it was a good one, wasn't it?" I said with a slight smirk in my voice, raising my eyebrows at her. "What about it?"

"Well, this may come as a shock to you, but I was totally into it and it made me think that I might like to try it."

"Try what?" I asked. Surely sweet, innocent, timid Sheila couldn't mean that she'd like to try kissing another woman!

"You know, *it*." (See, she couldn't even bring herself to say it.) "So I wanted to know if I could borrow some of your videos. You know, the adult ones." She paused, looking a little sheepish. In response to my skeptical look, she continued, "Well, I've never been into the thought of myself with another woman, you know that, I just never considered it before. I'd thought of it, but it never held any appeal for me. But last night it seemed different somehow, I was completely turned on, even imagining myself as Carla. That's never happened before, and I'm still thinking about it, and I figured that if I watched a porn video with women having sex I could figure out whether I'd really enjoy it or not. Sort of like a litmus test."

"Are you serious? You've never seemed interested in women in the least, and all of a sudden this show makes you want to be a lesbian? I know it was a sexy episode, but really!" I didn't know how to hide my shock, and I didn't want to offend her, but I was reeling. Sheila was one of my closest friends, and also one of the straightest. She was also pretty innocent about sexual matters in general and always seemed a bit unnerved when I related a tale of casual sex. For her, almost everything I did in my dating life was "scandalous." I knew she'd only slept with a handful of men, and that even though she'd had crushes, she rarely acted on them because she was always too nervous. Sheila was the kind of woman who always waits for the guy to make the first move.

"Well, everyone can try new things. I can't explain it, but watching that scene between those two women I got totally turned on. I just got swept away with it and really felt curious. I feel like something's changed for me, like I'm a slightly different person now, and I want to pursue that impulse. Oh, Rachel, don't look at me that way, I'm serious. I just feel like I have to explore this and find out more. Plus I've been totally horny since watching it and I need some release. It's been a long time."

"Well, I can give you some recommendations for videos, there are some excellent ones out now with really sexy actresses and hot scenes. Why can't you just go to the video store yourself and rent them?"

Suddenly, Sheila was back to her old, conservative self. "I could never do that, I'd be way too embarrassed. I'm curious, but not that curious. I really need your help! You must have some porn videos at home, so can't you just bring them?"

"Well, I'll do it, but just so you know, my videos aren't exactly top of the line. They're all kind of cheesy, and they really aren't going to give you a true picture of what it's like to have sex with a woman. In real life it's so much more intense and magical and beautiful than what's in my videos. My videos I got because they're cheap and are nice to look at, but they're full of clichés that usually make me laugh rather than turn me on. You'll really want something more real if you're using this to make such a big decision."

"No, no, they'll be fine. I just want to see naked women, up close, to really get a sense of what it's like. They don't have to be perfect. Please, just do this for me. I never ask you for anything, and this is really important. You're the only one I can talk to about this, and I really want to watch them."

I reluctantly agreed, and the next day I smuggled my three measly videos into work in a thick, sealed black bag so that nobody would know our dirty little secret. After lunch I thrust them at her as we were each going back to our desks.

She grabbed my arm. "But wait, I thought you would watch them with me."

As soon as she said that, everything changed. Instead of our usual teasing conversations about sex in all its varieties, we were entering a much more personal terrain. Telling her all about my lovers and much of my sex life is one thing; that's something women, both straight and queer, tend to do when they get together and talk. She would tell me of her escapades with her old boyfriend, in explicit detail, and I'd tell her my dating adventures, but I left more to the imagination than she did. I was just grateful to have someone to talk to at our mostly male office. It was never awkward; it was just girl talk.

But now I felt a weird charge in the air. I had no idea what to say or think. Did she mean that she just wanted me to pal along and enjoy the porn, or would I be part of her girl/girl experiment? The thought left me confused. In all the time I'd known her, through all the girlfriends and dates and sex I'd told her about, she'd listened patiently and offered advice when asked, but she'd never expressed more than a very casual interest in the idea of lesbian sex. In fact, if anything I'd sensed that when it came to my sex life she didn't want to know the details. Perhaps that had changed, thanks to prime time television. But how awkward! I wasn't even sure I was attracted to her, I'd never really given it any thought, and now I felt like I was part of some documentary: *The World of Lesbian Sex*.

Despite my uncertainty, I agreed—out of curiosity, thrill seeking, or lust, I'm not really sure. It just didn't seem like I could gracefully refuse, and her enthusiasm was endearing.

The next evening I knocked on her door at 9. She hurriedly ushered me in. I felt like we were on a date, which was such a crazy thought, but there was that same charge in the air, that anticipation of what will happen next and the knowledge that something definitely will. I felt like it was almost out of my hands now that I was there. After all, it's pretty rare that you watch a porn video with someone then just go on your way, commenting on the directing and acting as you would with a regular movie. I expected at least one of us to get turned on, but I didn't know who it would be or what would happen after that point. I'd almost called with an excuse. But then I told myself I didn't have anything to worry about; nothing would happen that I didn't want.

Sheila led me into the living room. We put the first movie in and she got comfortable on her bed while I sat near her on the floor. The movie started, and I tried to protest again that it really wasn't a representative sampling of lesbian lust, but she didn't seem to mind.

Instead of two hot, healthy women smoking up the screen, we watched these stringy-haired gals with huge boobs chatting each other up in the front office of a women's gym. I'd seen it before, and as I'd told Sheila earlier, I wasn't too impressed. I like my porn, but this was such a weak attempt I wondered if we'd even make it until the end. I couldn't really get into it, and was feeling a bit bored, but when I tried to protest, she gave me a look that told me this was important to her, beyond important, and she wanted lesbian porn, even if it was bad lesbian porn.

I kept watching, realizing there really wasn't anywhere else to look to ease the tension in the room. Aside from the noise from the video, the room was totally quiet. On the screen the two female gym employees stared down at their very slim clients, lifting their legs in syncopation. Slowly the two moved closer together, then they were kissing. "I've been waiting for this ever since you got here," said one of them, pulling the other toward her. Very soon they were on the floor of the office, behind the desk, naked. What a corny plotline!

Still, I kept watching as the woman who'd spoken was now eagerly parting the legs of the other woman, revealing a trimmed, pink, glistening pussy. "This is what I've missed," she said and stroked said glistening pussy up and down, tapping on her clit before starting to lick the woman's cunt like it was going out of style.

Despite my protests, I was getting turned on, and Sheila's chatter had also fallen away. I tried to sneak looks at her out of the corner of my eye, but she was transfixed. I was getting excited without even meaning to. I felt her move closer, but I just sat there, waiting to see what would happen. She'd been bold enough to ask me for the videos and practically demand that I watch them with her, and I wanted to see if she really wanted me enough to make the first move. Knowing she was so nervous made it even hotter.

Her hand grazed across my shoulder and I felt shivers run through my body. Here we were watching the rawest of sex acts—her hand brushing my shoulder almost gave me an orgasm. I felt myself holding my breath, which I do when I'm turned on. I didn't even realize it until I let out a huge breath and felt the desire travel through me. Her hand stayed on my shoulder, squeezing it. I could hear her breath.

As one of the women moved and began to lick the other's pussy, she whispered into my ear, "I like that." I closed my eyes, unable to look at the screen anymore. How could my simple, sweet friend Sheila be driving me so insane?

She lifted my hair and began to softly kiss the back of my

neck. I felt like I would explode. Tingling, almost ticklish sensations rose up on my skin. Her lips were hot and her eagerness excited me. She was usually so timid about sex, and here she was going after me, making me sizzle in places I'd all but forgotten about. When she licked my neck, I let out a breath that came out as a moan. She could tell she was having an effect on me. She kissed my cheek, then slid off the bed and onto the floor. She crawled like a cat to the TV, shutting it off.

She crawled back, a predatory smile on her face. "I want to make you come." From anyone else, it might have sounded fake or trite, but she said it with such seriousness I couldn't resist. I had expected to come here and humor her, maybe even make out a little, but I'd never expected to be so aroused. She approached and spread my legs apart, settling herself in between them. As I leaned against the bed for support, she writhed on top of me.

I couldn't stand it anymore. I lifted her up and lay her down across the bed, then positioned myself on top of her. "So, you like what you saw there, did you? You want to see how juicy and wet and hot a girl like me can be?" She nodded. "Well, maybe I want to do the same thing to you." I pushed her legs apart and pushed my knee against her very wet center. She closed her eyes and moaned, pushing back against me. I began toying with one hard nipple, then the other, through her flimsy shirt. She rocked on the bed.

"Are you ready for me, baby?" I asked.

We were no longer Sheila and Rachel, office gossip buddies, but in our own exalted porn world, where our relationship took on new complexities. She didn't look innocent to me anymore as she lay across the bed, daring me to take her to new places and show her body hidden delights.

I spread her legs apart and stroked her with my fingers. Then I inched my way under her panties to find her totally hot and eager. Two fingers entered her easily and I pushed against her yearning pussy. When I pulled my fingers out a few minutes later, she grabbed my wrist, urging me back inside her. I resisted her though and brought my fingers up to her mouth so she could taste herself. She suckled on my fingers before gently biting them. I returned the favor by wrapping my lips around her nipple, sucking it hard. We each sucked and teethed on our respective treats. Then she pulled me to her and kissed me deeply. She looked up at me. "Rachel, you are so amazing. This is perfect."

I kissed her back, amazed that something this unexpected could feel so good. I made my way back to her pussy, which was still wet and waiting for more attention. I inched her panties down with my teeth until I couldn't wait any longer and yanked them the rest of the way with my hands. Then I leaned down to caress her with my tongue, plunging it inside her, tasting her, feeling her writhe underneath me. As I circled her clit with my tongue, I used my fingers inside her to get her even more excited. "That's good, that's perfect, Rachel, don't stop," she moaned as I sped up the pace of my fingers and tongue. I could feel her squirming, getting ready to come, and held on tighter. When she came she pushed her pelvis upward, so my tongue stayed firmly on her clit. She let out a huge sigh, and I gently pulled out of her, my wet fingers feeling cool in the air. I didn't want to stop, to remove myself from the trance of fucking her, to bring us back to some other space, where we were neither lovers, nor friends, but some strange, uncertain combination of the two. I lay my head down against her hip and let her hand play with my hair. Neither of us wanted to resolve our gloriously complicated relationship until the morning. I turned, glanced at the VCR and the long-forgotten video, smiled, and closed my eyes.

The One

WARNER WILLIAMS

Her name was Lorraine. She was tall and had—to coin a phrase—legs to die for. She had the body of a model, perfection at its best. She was my first. My first what? My first everything. My first kiss, my first girlfriend, and my first teacher—and, God knows, I was in dire need of some teaching.

I was 23 when I first met Lorraine, at a nightclub called Masquerades. When she walked in the door, there was just something about her that grabbed me right between the legs. She wore a very tight blouse with an extremely low neckline. Her breasts seemed to signal like two burning beacons on a pitch-black night. Her curves were like a long stretch of highway, a wild joyride I'd take with the pedal to the metal and the top down. But what caught my eye most was the way she walked in her miniskirt, the swing of those long, beautiful legs that ended in three-inch spiked heels.

She found a table not far from the door and sat down, not seeming at all comfortable there alone. I couldn't take my eyes off her, and sometimes it was as though she felt my stare and would look up at me. Like a child I'd look away and pretend I wasn't staring.

At that time in my life I was a pro at flirting then running for the hills once the hunt began. How else could I have stayed a virgin for so long? I guess that night my hormones finally told me that enough was enough—or maybe it was the tequila. Whichever it was, I finally got up the nerve.

First I walked over to the pool table and pretended to watch the game to compose myself, trying to think of some not-so-worn-out line to impress her. Over at the banister behind her table was my next move, but then it hit me. What if she wasn't cool? So there I stood, silently praying, *Please let her be cool, please let her be cool, or at least normal.* Finally I took a breath and held it. My insides screamed at me like a deranged drill sergeant: *I'm not going to let you breathe until you go over there!* So I did, and out came the words: "Would you like to dance?"

Would you like to dance?

Those were the only words I could say after practicing all that time? I couldn't believe them as they came from my mouth. I was in a state of shock. It was turning out that I was the uncool one.

And then I heard: "I was wondering how long it would take you to walk over here."

I laughed out loud, relieved at the sudden ease I felt with her. She didn't want to dance, something about not liking the song. Instead she invited me to sit down, and as I stared at her innocent, dreamy eyes she told me how she hated being out alone.

Of course, my lame reply was, "A beautiful woman like you shouldn't have to be."

She replied that it was a long story and she'd explain it to me another time. As she spoke, she put her glass to her lips, caressing them with its edge and looking so deeply into my eyes I felt she'd touched my soul. We left the club, going our separate ways after exchanging numbers in the parking lot.

I was a senior in college and had finals coming up, but intrusive thoughts of her made studying impossible. For the next two days and nights in a row, I did nothing but wait for the phone to ring. Finally I broke down and called her. That night we had dinner and got to know each other better. I couldn't believe it when this total femme told me she was a sergeant in the military! I hesitated to tell Lorraine about myself—yes, the one and only 23-year-old virgin. She told me she thought this was something that made me very special, but she didn't look at me when she said it. Clearly, it made her nervous.

Time and time again, date after date, it was torture. Seeing but not touching. Touching but not tasting. I was glad I wasn't a guy, because if I'd had a set of balls they'd have been blue. One night as we talked on the phone she admitted that my being a virgin made her nervous. "I just think your first time should be really special, and I afraid I'd mess it up."

"I don't understand," I told her. "Being with you *would* be special."

We didn't talk about it any more that night, and it would be days before she called asking me to come over and hang out.

When I arrived at her house, I couldn't believe the heat as I got out of my car. With my shirt clinging to my back, I walked to her door and rung the bell. It seemed to take her forever, but when she opened the door I decided it had been well worth the wait. I closed my eyes and slowly opened them again. Was I really seeing what I was seeing? It was hot outside, but I knew it was going to be even hotter inside!

There stood the teacher of all teachers dressed in a tight,

white cut-off tank top designed to show off a gorgeous, smooth-skinned midriff. Her hard, round nipples peeked tantalizingly through the flimsy material. My eyes followed the curves of her waist down to an unbuttoned, half-unzipped pair of crotch-hugging blue jean shorts. Her perfume enticed and enveloped me like the potent melody of a snake charmer.

I walked in not knowing what to expect or what to do. She saw my nervousness and grabbed my hand, pulling me close, then slammed the door behind us as she embraced me with a full, hypnotizing kiss. She held my face in her hands then kissed me again, this time in a prolonged tease of soft lips and surging bites. I wanted to caress her, but I wasn't sure of exactly how to go about it. Lorraine smiled in a very sexy and reassuring way that said, *Don't worry. I will show you how.*

She led me to the couch and sat me there, then turned from me and lowered herself softly onto my lap. Taking my hands in hers, she wrapped them around her shoulders at first then, like water flowing, guided them over every contour of her body. My fingertips found themselves bombarded with sensation as the exploration washed slowly down her soft supple neck, then chest, resting at her breasts. Her hard nipples pushed against the palms of my hands, seemingly begging for attention as she made small circles around them with our hands. My hands met the curves of her thighs, and each new caress was like a baptism leading to the golden doors of heaven. She ran my fingers along the outer edges then along the tops of her thighs, each time coming closer to the center of ecstasy.

At last she freed my hands, which instinctively followed the invisible tracks she had traced only seconds before.

Now there was no forbidden zone. I let my fingers explore, running them across the seam of her cut-offs, searching for a reaction. I dipped my hand inside her unzipped shorts and erased all barriers between us. Her lips were warm and wet, and with every touch I could feel her excitement build. The more I explored, the wider her legs spread, the more she slid forward, and the heavier her breath sounded in my ear. I traced her wetness then entered her, softly at first, then rapid and hard as her body writhed and bucked.

Teasingly I stopped for a moment, then returned to her clit, which throbbed and swelled as I ran my fingers around it over and over. I was no longer able to resist and pressed its center while, with my free hand, I massaged her breast in the same small circular motion. Lorraine's passion intensified. I thought she'd come at any moment, but instead she grabbed my hand and gasped, "Wait!"

Lorraine rose, taking me by the hand like a child, and led me to the bedroom, where rows of glimmering candles encircled the bed. She stood before me, taking off her shirt, and I ran my fingers down to remove her shorts. The world outside stood still—all that existed was our touch, our kisses, and the sound of my own heartbeat. Slowly she undressed me, her motions a mesmerizingly exotic dance. Unbuttoning my shirt. Running her nails up my back to remove my bra. Pinching my hard, eager nipples. I exhaled passionately. Once I was completely undressed she lay back on the bed, again guiding my motions with her hands. She spread her legs apart and directed my hips between them, grabbing my ass to rock me hard against her wetness. As I listened to the unspoken language of her body my motions became hers, and hers mine. We moved as one, our bodies merged together in passion.

Our bodies were indistinguishable. Our sweat poured down to the sheets beneath us. There was so much more I wanted to know, to explore. I broke her embrace and began to trace her body with my tongue. The saltiness of her sweat and the sweet scent of her perfume guided me through the unknown. I took her nipple inside my mouth and sucked hard as I caressed it with my tongue. She moaned in ecstasy. The energy surged through me like a spark down my spine, setting my every nerve on fire.

I kissed and tongued my way down her stomach, my breath hot on her skin until finally I was there. Her scent possessed me. I had the uncontrollable urge to taste her, to feel her lose control inside my mouth. Suddenly she became silent. I parted her lips and ran my tongue across her wet clit. She clawed the sheets as she fought to contain her moans. With her warm clit in my mouth, I sucked gently at first, then harder. Overcome with passion, I grabbed her thighs. A sound rose in her throat—almost like a cry; I stopped for a moment and nervously asked, "Did I hurt you?" She looked into my eyes lovingly and shook her head; then she smiled and ran her fingers through my hair, guiding me back to her quivering clit.

My body throbbed with the excitement of a ticking bomb. She grabbed at my hair and pulled me into her. Then she completely lost control, and the room filled with her loud sobs of pleasure.

Somewhere between her cries and mine, our bodies merged in ecstasy. There were no words for the peace I had found. I opened my eyes and found my angel beckoning me to hold her. Our lips met, we embraced, and the sweetness of her in my ear was all I heard. She rolled over and I curled up behind her, my arms never wanting to let her go. She whispered to me softly, the sound of exhaustion in her voice, "Your first time. Yeah, right! You were too good for me to believe that."

But it *was* my first time—and one I will never forget.

Lust to Love

MIA DOMINGUEZ

I was a very innocent lesbian. Of course, I had experience, and the desire to explore and delve into my personal fantasies, but I had no idea what I was missing until I met Rebecca—though I was still sticking it out with Annie at the time.

One evening as Annie and I lay in bed discussing our nonexistent sex life, I made up my mind to move on:

"I talked to my therapist today," she said.

"About what?"

"About us. Actually, about our sex life."

"What sex life?"

"That's what I mean. We're having some sex problems, and I wanted to discuss them with her."

"What gives you the right to discuss my personal life with a stranger?"

"She's not a stranger. She's my therapist, and I needed to talk to her about our problems."

"What problems do we have anyway?" I demanded. "It seems to me the only problems we have are the ones you manufacture so we won't have sex."

"She says you're too aggressive for me and that you need to let me make the first move sometimes."

I laughed. "If I waited around for you to make the first

move we'd never have sex. I can't wait forever, until you get over whatever is going on with you." I took a moment to collect myself. "Look, Annie, we only have a few months invested in this, and I have nothing against you, but I really don't feel that we can have a decent relationship without having a decent sex life. I can't, anyway."

"Is that all you think about?" she accused.

"No, but I'm not going to deny the importance of it either." I grabbed a cigarette from my purse and lit it up.

"I asked you not to smoke around me, Mia."

"I asked you to make love to me, *Annie,* and you can't or won't or don't know how. In any case, look, I think we should date other women. I think we'll find out that we really don't belong together—and how bad would it be if we each found someone a little more compatible?"

"You're fucked." Annie started to cry.

"No, I'm *not* fucked, and it doesn't look like I'm going to get fucked anytime soon. Not by you anyway." I sat on the bed, frustrated and tired, needing to put an end to our disagreement so I could get some sleep. "I need to tell you something."

"What is it?"

"I've met someone else." I saw the look on her face. The look that showed she was preparing to go ballistic on me, so I interrupted her. "Before you say anything, I want you to know that I haven't physically cheated on you. I placed an ad in the personals and I was waiting to see who answered, and after talking to a couple of women I've found someone I'd really like to meet in person."

"Go to hell, Mia! How could you do this to me?"

"Well, what the hell am I supposed to do? Be celibate because my girlfriend won't touch me? I don't want to be with someone who has to speak to her therapist before deciding whether it's OK to have sex. I want passion. I want to be desired. I want to be swept off my feet. I don't want to be summoned to a therapy session with my girlfriend of three months. That doesn't work for me."

"Mia, it has nothing to do with me not being attracted to you. It has everything to do with me. I'm the one with the problem."

"If you're the one with the problem, why are you discussing me with your therapist? Why is your therapist having you tell me I have to let you make the first move?" I was tired of her back-pedaling. "It's over, Annie. You may not agree with me right now, but it's the best thing to do. If we don't break up now, we'll end up hating each other."

"Are you going to date this other woman?"

"Yes, I think so."

"Do you like her?"

"I've never even seen her. We've only spoken on the phone."

"While you've been with me?"

"Yes. I'm sorry, Annie. I only decided that I wanted to meet her in person last night, and that's why I needed to talk to you. I am trying to be honest."

"I better go now," Annie whispered. She picked up the bits and pieces of her clothing left around my bedroom. The jeans hanging over the desk chair, her robe on the hook over the door, a couple of T-shirts in my drawer. She pulled the pair of jeans on over her pajama pants, grabbed her shoes, and headed for the door. "Guess I'll see you around."

"Bye, Annie." I didn't offer any more condolences, because I simply wanted all of this to come to the quickest ending possible. I may sound like the biggest asshole ever, but I wasted no time in calling Rebecca and setting up a date.

That Saturday night, I couldn't wait for Rebecca to walk up to my door. I was dying to see what she looked like. When I heard her truck drive up I peeked out the window and caught the most beautiful glimpse of my future. She looked exactly as I had imagined her looking as we spoke on the phone each night, and exactly like the woman I had fantasized about as I attempted to find sleep. I burned with lust. My only concern was that she might not feel for me what I now felt for her. Those prolonged seconds of the walk from her truck to my front door were filled with anticipation. It was the first time I felt insecure about myself, and it was the most uncomfortable feeling I'd experienced in a long time.

Finally, she knocked on the door. I waited a few seconds, so as not to appear desperate, then opened it. "Hi."

She smiled. "Hi. Is Mia home?"

I laughed. "I'm Mia. Rebecca, right?"

"That's me. My God," she sighed, "I knew you'd be attractive, especially from your description, but you are really gorgeous."

She touched my face.

"I can't tell you how many times I've been disappointed in these kind of meetings," I said.

"Well, I hope you're not disappointed now, honey, because I'm in heaven." She hugged me.

"I'm absolutely not disappointed. This is the best blind date I've ever had, and it hasn't even started yet."

We laughed, and she asked, "So, did you decide what you'd like to do yet?"

"No. I thought you might have something in mind."

"Well, I saw that cute Italian place when I got off the freeway. Would you like to have a nice dinner and maybe share a bottle of wine?"

"Sure. Let me go get my purse, and we can go." I walked into the bedroom, straightened out the bed, fluffed the pillows, threw the clothes from the floor into the closet, picked up my purse, then went back into the living room.

"Are you ready?" I asked.

"Yeah." Rebecca got up from the sofa and grabbed my arm. "Let's go, baby."

Just as I was about to open the door, Rebecca swung me around, pressed my back against it, and kissed me. What I thought was going to be a sweet little introductory kiss turned into a long make-out session. Rebecca touched me over my clothes and, with little or no direction (and no resistance from me either), did whatever else she wanted. She unbuttoned my shirt halfway and buried her face in my cleavage. I loved it! I held her head down as she searched for my nipples and ran her hands up my shorts. Finally, I couldn't take any more.

"What's wrong, baby?"

"Nothing's wrong. Come with me." I took her hand and led her into my bedroom.

We immediately fell onto the bed. Rebecca was so desperate to get back to my tits, she didn't bother unbuttoning the rest of my shirt. She just tore it open.

"I'm sorry, Mia. I'll take you shopping," she said as she ripped off whatever was left of my shirt.

"Don't worry about it," I answered passionately. I ran my hands up her T-shirt, wanting to feel her, and she backed away from me.

LUST TO LOVE

"Don't do that," she said.

"Why not?"

"I don't know. I just don't like people playing with my tits."

"Are you kidding me?"

"No."

Thoughts of Annie flooded my brain.

"That's bullshit." I pulled her onto the bed, and I threw myself on top of her. "Don't put restrictions on me, Rebecca. If you want all of me, you have to give me all of you." I lifted up her shirt, grabbing her soft mounds and filling my mouth up with her beautiful caramel flesh. She held me tight while I feasted on her plump breasts.

"You can't put restrictions on me either, Mia."

"I won't."

"Promise?"

"I promise."

"We're gonna have a lot of fun together," Rebecca whispered in my ear before she rolled me over on my back and forced her head between my legs. She tenderly brushed her lips along my thighs, then stopped to meet my wet, anxious pussy lips, parting them with her warm fingers as her tongue probed my swollen clit. *What am I doing?* I wondered. *This woman is having her way with me, and I hardly even know her.* But I didn't care if we'd known each other for 10 days or 10 minutes, I had already surrendered myself—with no restrictions.

Rebecca and I spent hours in bed, playing and exploring each other's bodies, then resting up for more. It was getting late and suddenly we were starving, so we ordered Chinese food and decided to get to know each other better while we waited.

"Are you disappointed?" Rebecca asked.

"Not at all. Why do you ask?"

"Because I know you're a good girl." She touched my cheek.

"What makes you think I'm a good girl?"

"I just know you are, that's all."

"Is that a bad thing?"

"Not as long as you're willing to be naughty with me."

"I am being naughty with you."

"I know—and I love it. I want to show you so many things and make you feel incredible, but I want to be the only one." Rebecca slipped her hand inside my robe and fondled my breast. "I want you to be mine. I want you to only want and long for me. Can you do that?"

"Yes, I can. I want to." Once again I felt hot; I needed another dose of her to hold me over until dinner.

By the end of the night, I guess it was official: I was Rebecca's girlfriend, and she was mine. We belonged to each other, and I loved it. We saw each other every night, and every night we shared another fantasy. Even on the nights we had promised to give ourselves a break, as soon as one called the other to say good night, it was only a matter of minutes before we'd work ourselves into a frenzy and one would be summoned to tuck the other in properly. We couldn't keep our hands off each other. Still, Rebecca continued to hint at certain "things" that she wanted to show me. Things she knew I hadn't been exposed to.

One night, as we lay in bed, I decided to ask her.

"When you said you wanted to show me new things, what did you mean?"

"Are you serious?" Rebecca laughed. "Do you want me to tell you or show you?"

"What do you want to do?"

"I want to show you." Rebecca kissed me hard and seductively, then got out of bed, saying, "I'll be back."

"Where are you going?"

"To the rest room. I'll be back in a minute." Rebecca turned the light switch off before she closed the door behind her. I lay in bed and wondered what she was doing in there. There was no water running, the toilet didn't flush. There wasn't much movement in there at all—and the more I tried to listen, the quieter it got. When I heard the doorknob, I lay back in bed casually. Rebecca climbed into bed and resumed making out with me. She pulled herself on top of me, and something hard touched my leg.

"If I'm not making you feel good, just tell me and I'll stop, OK?"

"OK, hon."

Rebecca kissed me hard, then slowly worked her way down my cheek, my neck, my breasts. She grew more intense and passionate as the excitement escalated between us. I became wet knowing what was between her legs, and instantly heated when she spread my knees apart and plunged herself between them. I winced aloud.

"Are you OK, baby?" she asked.

"Yeah, I'm OK."

"Why'd you make that sound?"

"It feels good."

"You like it?"

"I like it a lot."

Rebecca was the only woman I'd ever done this with, and my obvious enjoyment of the experience unleashed a frenzy of lust. She plunged her thick dildo in and out till I creamed on her over and over again. I was hot and naughty and wanted to thrill her. I flipped our positions and began to ride. My tits danced wildly as I slid up and down on her slippery hot toy. I pinned her arms. My hard nipples brushed her face.

"Mia, you're driving me crazy," she whispered in my ear.

"I want to drive you crazy, baby."

That night we realized we would never tire of each other. I had promised Rebecca no restrictions and would continue to keep my word.

With the exception of my brief relationship with Annie, I'd had a great sex life before I met Rebecca. Although it was quite tame, it satisfied me, because I never realized just how tame it was. But now that I had met Rebecca, I'd never be able to find satisfaction with what she called "vanilla sex" again. I was addicted to her and her voracious appetite for the new, the darker, and the deeper side of sensuality, and I craved the unexpected surprises she continued to have waiting for me over the next four years.

A perfect example happened during the first month we lived together. I came home from work one night wanting nothing more than to crash till the next morning. I didn't care about dinner or bathing or anything. I just needed to sleep. When I walked inside—although Rebecca's truck was parked in the garage—it was pitch-black in the house. At the very moment I went for the light switch, someone grabbed my hand and covered my mouth. I was scared until I realized it was only Rebecca playing the role of an assailant.

She was rough and forceful with me, reaching underneath the skirt of my business suit and ripping my panties right off. She pulled the jacket off my back and forced her hands underneath my bra, releasing my breasts, grabbing them with authority, and biting my nipples. Every time I screamed, she bit down harder and grabbed me tighter. It was heaven.

When Rebecca discovered that I knew it was she who had grabbed me, and that I was a willing participant in whatever she had in mind, she kissed me passionately, then stopped, flung me over the sofa, tied my hands behind my back, and spanked me. I screamed. Not even in my childhood did I receive such a beating.

"Stop!" I screamed.

"You don't want me to stop, do you?" Rebecca gave me another swat. "Doesn't that feel good?"

"No, honey," I complained. "It hurts."

Rebecca would have none of it. She rubbed my ass as if to apologize, then laid another one—a harder one—on me. This time I felt it all over. My pussy began to cream. I moaned, succumbing to her prowess.

"Do you really want me to stop?"

"No, baby," I answered.

"What do you want?" she asked, rubbing her hands across my ass.

"Spank me, baby," I begged. "I want you to hurt me."

Rebecca obliged me. And with every strike of her hand on my flesh, I became more aroused. She was shirtless, but wearing her jeans, and as she rubbed up against my ass I realized she was packing.

"Are you OK, baby?"

"Yes."

"I love you."

"I love you, too."

"No restrictions, right?"

"No, baby. No restrictions."

"Good." She put me on my knees, then pulled something from her back pocket and used it as a blindfold to cover my eyes. I heard her zipper. Rebecca ran her hands through my long, curly hair, then caressed my head and touched my lips. Then I felt something else touch my lips. It was hard and cold, and although my hands were tied behind my back and my eyes covered, I knew it was hers, and I opened my mouth to take it. Rebecca thrust her hips slowly and gently into my mouth as I performed for her just the way she wanted me to. I ran my tongue up and down the shaft of our toy, showing my appreciation for all she'd done for me with it.

Just knowing that once again I hadn't rejected her brought us closer. Rebecca joined me on the floor, pulled the blindfold from my eyes, and unbound my hands.

"What's the matter?" I asked, concerned because the mood suddenly became serious.

"I'm in love with you," she confessed.

"Is that a bad thing?"

"No, it's a beautiful thing. I'm sorry if I ever made you do anything you didn't want to do."

"If I didn't want to do it, I wouldn't have."

"You seemed so innocent when I met you, now I feel that I've spoiled you."

"I've enjoyed exploring with you. I've enjoyed every minute of it. Trust me. This has been the best experience of my life."

"Really?"

"Yes," I answered. "I love being with you. It makes me feel alive and human and I want to experience everything with you before we die or get too old to do it anymore."

We laughed, knowing that we both had truly met our match. There was no need for guilt or shame. Our relationship, born from lust, grew into something deep and loving, and even though it's been over for several years now, I look back fondly on those days, and I have to thank her for giving me the best education a girl could have.

She made it possible for me to introduce many women to the same caliber of pleasure.

Fist

CANDICE GIDEON

Tonight I am staring at your hands, hypnotized. You have been talking animatedly, gesturing with your strong, capable, expressive hands about the new piece you are working on. Your eyes are dark with the promise of art and passion and, after a slow sip of wine, you set the glass down, its deep burgundy shining in the candlelight, and you show me what you are discovering in the wood. One hand makes a fist and the other rests under it to show me the emerging shape. My sudden intake of breath startles you, and you stop—but before you can move those hands I put my smaller ones around your fist and hold it, gently lay my forehead on it, then bring my lips to it. Your fist is warm and strong; I let my lips softly trace each curved finger to the knuckle, then I just rest my mouth there and whisper against it...

"Please."

That ragged little whisper undoes you. I hear your breath catch as you gently uncurl your fingers and lay your palm flat against my cheek.

You lean in to kiss me, pulling my lower lip into your mouth, gently biting it. Then you kiss me the way you do—your lips traveling mine, so certain and bold, pulling me into a soft, pliant, hungry place, sweet with the tender ache of wanting. You pull away and look into my eyes, your voice soft and low...

"Why...? Why is this so important to you, baby?"

The question demands the truth of an answer. My eyes close as you pull me onto your lap. I swing my leg over you, straddling you face to face, feeling your hard thighs against my own. My lips find yours, and your hands move over me, searching out the spots that make me sigh into your mouth, and when I feel your hand between my legs I shiver. You hold your familiar hand balled into an unmistakable, unfamiliar fist between my legs, and I move against it, frustrated by the layer of denim.

You press your fist there, hard against me, and you tilt your head back so you can see my eyes and ask me again...

"Why is this so important to you?"

I am sorry that you ask. I just want to close my eyes and feel that fist of yours, imagine it inside me. "It's the last innocent thing I own."

"What?" You sound puzzled, but you do not move. You are listening to me with all of yourself, giving me your complete attention. I am suddenly aware of the quiet in the room, the flicker of candlelight casting shadows up all around us.

My mouth goes dry. "Your fist...inside me..." I pause and close my eyes again for a moment, feeling you watch me. "You fucking me with your fist." I move against it as I say the words. "This is the last virgin thing I have, perhaps the only virgin thing I have ever had, and I want to give it to you, I want you to take it." I shiver, feeling so naked despite my clothes. Sitting over you, your fist balled up against the creased crotch of my jeans.

You do not move your fist, but whisper, "What if...?"

and I can feel your kind concern for me, your worry for me, my history coming in. An unwelcome compassion.

I put my lips over yours and kiss you, wrap my arms around your neck, and move again against your fist. As my lips trail down to your throat, I whisper, "You won't hurt me…please…I need you to take the one thing no one ever stole from me…please." My voice is soft and husky as I beg you with it, not just with words but with the sound, not just with the sound but with my hips pressing me even harder against your fist.

"Please, I need you…"

I feel the heat of your response, and you are stroking me now, touching me, kissing me hungrily, and there is the rapid sound of movement, the noise of things falling, and suddenly I find myself lying on the dining room table you built with your own hands—my hips almost at the edge. I can't track what's happening, only that you have unzipped my jeans and pulled them down around my ankles. You are leaning over me, kissing me hard, and each place you touch sparks to a low fire, your hands roaming, finding each secret spot that aches for you. You pull my jeans off and run your hands slowly up my legs. You stroke my tender inner thighs, which open for you, and I gaze at your face looking back at me, at all of me, with that sweet, hungry knowing, that cocky delight I love so much.

You have a little smile at the corners of your mouth as you look into my eyes then let your eyes travel down me; as your eyes reach my breasts your hands slide up to unbutton my shirt and then you are cupping my breasts and lightly stroking my nipples as I arch my back. You capture each nipple between thumb and forefinger, pinch and roll them, then pull them toward your lips. When your warm mouth settles over my right breast, I moan a little, one hand making a fist, holding on to my composure, while the other wanders through your short, spiky hair.

You are on point right now, your lips, teeth, and tongue all dancing around my nipple, teasing, wetting, and biting until I am shivering. My juices run down onto the wood table as you slide your right hand over my clit, over my lips, your fingers dipping into my wetness, then sliding up my belly, leaving a little damp trail to evaporate from my hot skin. I feel those fingers at my mouth, running over my lips teasingly then resting on my bottom lip until I open my mouth and you slip your fingers inside and I am tasting my own wetness on top of the familiar smoky-sweet taste of your fingers.

I suck your fingers and whimper. This is how you like me to be: pliable, wet with hunger, incoherent with need. You release my right nipple and move to my left. Your mouth moves hard and fast on my nipple. You pull it between your teeth and bite it, then pull it deeply into your mouth, sucking hard as you move your fingers, hard, in and out of my mouth. Your other hand balls itself into a fist, and that fist rests up against the opening of my cunt and I grow weak with the feel of it there, and I suck harder on your fingers.

I am all ache. Wide open places needing you. I am a fat purple blossom dripping with need, opening to you. You take your fingers from my mouth and trace them straight down to my belly, to my thighs. Your fist slides down to rest against the table, up against my ass as you slip those two fingers—wet with me, wet from my mouth—inside of me in one hard push and I cry out as hot, wet waves roll through me. I take a long shaky breath to calm down and you slide those two fingers in and out a few times, then you run them from pussy to ass and I can feel your fist again right at the opening of my cunt, which is so wet that your fist is wet from the contact and you slowly slide it up and down my pussy lips. Those same two fingers slip dripping down to my ass. I am so wet that we don't need lube, that I don't want lube. I want to feel every single sensation.

When you slide both fingers into my ass, my cunt spasms on itself, clenching down on its own empty ache, and I moan and move my hips against the table, moving my wet cunt against your closed fist. I am begging you now, and I hear you whisper...

"OK, baby...open up for me...more."

I do, throwing open not just my legs, not just my cunt, but a long shuttered window inside my chest, something nailed down and shut tight over the years—and now the light just rushes in.

There is a sharp little growl in your throat. "Spread your legs wider for me." And those words and your tone make me wild with wanting, with hunger for you.

And I comply so that my thigh muscles are shaking. I am waiting to feel your fingers—instead I feel a wet warmth, a flicker of touch, and I realize you have settled your mouth over my clit. Your tongue gently strokes and slides, my hips roll down till they are pressed flat against the table, and I grow quiet, listening to the song you pull from me with your mouth, the little cries and moans.

You slip your tongue inside me. Soon I feel the slow unfolding of your fist against me till your palm is flat over my wet cunt. A single finger slips inside me and your tongue slides out to settle again at my clit, licking and sucking, and I sigh with relief. I am so wet that your finger freely slips around until you add a second finger. When you do, your fingers move in and out of me...in and out and I am gasping. I want to move, but you stop me.

"Lie still for me... Hold still."

Your voice is deep and low and fierce and I can feel how focused you are. Gratefully, I feel the third finger slip inside me. You move them in and out, my wetness running down to my ass and onto our dining room table.

I realize I have had my hands down at my inner thighs, as if to pull myself even more open for you. This ache I feel—not just in my cunt, but in my chest, in the exact center of me—this ache is almost too much to bear. I feel the fourth finger slip in. All of your fingers are slipping in and out...and your hand with each push is slipping in farther. One, two, three, four fingers slipping deeper and deeper inside. I'm aware of every detail of each finger, each knuckle, even the slight callus on a fingertip. My eyes close, and I am so still and quiet inside, feeling my pounding heart and liquid response to you, the wash of energy rushing through me in sweet, tender, exquisite waves. Yet, still, that enormous ache.

All my thoughts have now died down, and I only exist in your touch. Your fingers wind their way into me, catching all of my secrets, and I just open and open... There is a moment of sting, as you tuck your thumb under to work on slipping your whole hand inside. I welcome the sting—it's proof that this is a new gift, a virgin gift, and I have waited a lifetime to give it up, to give it to a woman like you.

And just now, just there... "Oh!" I cry as your hand slips all the way in, where it rests a moment, still. My breath startles out. I'm breathless, shivering on the edge of sharp, raw orgasm. My eyes open—yours are looking right at me. Your fist is inside of me. I am relieved to see heat in your eyes and hunger. As you slowly move your fist I cry out and shudder and there are tears welling in my eyes, an ocean rising in my cunt like a kind of baptism, a cleansing of all my old scars and suffering, a cleansing of all the things taken from me before I could even name them.

Your fist moves in me, pulling me closer, pushing me back...my hips are moving now...my feet braced against the table...I rise up to meet your hand buried in me...making noises now, singing you the strangest songs...my throat opening up to you just like the rest of me.

I ride your fist. You have finally taken what I have saved away secretly for years, watching women, eyeing their hands speculatively, searching their characters to see if this moment should belong to one of them.

And as your fist moves harder in me, you know I want, need, hunger for this hard fucking, I am moving now, riding it, riding your hand, moving with you. The tears of sweet relief pour down my face and I can see, when my eyes open, sweat on your chest through your white tank top. You are working hard, moving that fist in deep and then deeper until there is no part of my cunt that is not clamped down on your hand up to your wrist, a little more even...and as you pump your fist harder and faster, fucking me hard with your hand clutched tight in a fist, I start to come. A wild cry rushes up through me from my cunt through my belly to my throat—a deep achy wail.

You pump harder and as I come I cry out your name and I hear you whisper huskily as you keep pumping me, "That's it, sweet baby...let it all go, give it all up...come on..."

I do and the next is already building, the sweat starting to roll down your neck, my tears falling again. The whole room is full of the echo of sweat dripping, my slick come running down your wrist and between my legs; the smell of salt and fire and sawdust, spilled red wine; the heat—and the sweetest sounds of all are my dying cries as this orgasm shudders through me. Then, sweeter still, your answering moan, deep in your throat, your fist fucking me, the way I open to you, the feel of all that moisture, your own hunger...something tender and hard pushes you to your own edge and I know I have made you wet, too, that your kindness is resting somewhere quietly but in this moment you are here fucking me hard with all of you, with nothing held back. I am open to you, all of me. Nothing is hidden. As you slow your fist down, now moving it slowly around the walls and flesh of my cunt, gently moving it in and out, slow, steady, easy fucking. You look at me with a fierce sort of tenderness. As you move closer, leaning in to kiss me, your tongue slides inside my mouth and all history fades away. There is only the story we tell each other now, a story rich in touch, a flurry of colors, berry-stained mouths, the clean white hardness of sharp teeth, the strange dance of tongues singing our own rich songs as we cry out into each other's mouth, the scent of moisture in the air, the mystery of sawdust, the feel of your fist claiming my cunt for its own.

Behind the Propane Tank

SHAR REDNOUR

The '80s sure don't seem like 15-plus years ago. I mean, how can I have been legal that long? There are a couple of great things about the '80s. One is the eye shadow, of course—saturated hues and emboldened shapes that spilled your eyes past your temples and beyond your brows. I've been quoted a few times on that one. Who needs a Picasso when you can go out on the town with a work of art on your eyelids? I could get high and paint in plum-colored powders all day.

The other historical moment of value is that miniskirts came back. Unlike nowadays, when hemlines go up and down and up again faster than Oprah at a Celine Dion concert—in the '80s the world had seen neither hide nor hair of a miniskirt in over a decade. Even the idea of the mini received wide debates, with several women forcibly coming out against thigh exposure. "I don't care if everyone wears one, I won't be caught dead showing my legs like that." This is a direct quote from an—at that time—skinny, young, sexy friend of mine. No lie.

I waited impatiently—huffing and puffing in my local mall, cursing the local merchandisers—for the coastal trends to geriatrically creep to Illinois. The second they did I bought any mini I could afford. I had the unfortunate red tiered cotton one with a red-and-white-striped shirt to match (à la Whitney Houston in "I Wanna Dance with Somebody"), then I got a straight gray leather one, and a white fake leather one with supercool paisley embossing.

It was the gray leather skirt that I chose to wear to my first lesbian wedding. I matched it with a cotton shirt—pink dashed with squiggles of white—that I'd ripped and hemmed straight up the back so it swung open, revealing my lovely spine. The front I buttoned all the way up, and I added a thin gray-with-tiny-white-polka-dots leather tie. My perfectly spiked, bleached hair was done by Jimmy, the second most coveted stylist in Southern Illinois. And, the crème de la crème, Bette and Ranelle got married on a hot summer day so I had the perfect excuse to wear my purple and black swoosh sunglasses—you know, the ones in all those music videos? One side started out in a point that widened over the eyes into a jagged flash, as though an artist had captured a purple lightning bolt and transformed it into shades. I made sure I owned a pair, but I rarely had an occasion bold enough for them. This wedding would be that bold.

We were in the backyard of the tristate-famous drag queen Blanche Du Bois, who allowed her backyard to be transformed into a queer sanctuary replete with a floral archway. Blanche loved transformation. Her trailer served as everything from makeup room to event headquarters, with only wedding-party members allowed. There were "strict orders" about this, and you know how queens love to enforce strict orders to ensure quality glamour, sufficient surprise factor, and a sense of hierarchy. There are the mamas and the babies, and the lines are clear.

My closest friends were Brian and Steve. We'd all gone

to high school with Bette, who was my age. Normally, the boys and I were connected at the hip, but since I'm a year older than they are I was the only one who'd just finished a year of college—a year as a vampire, so to speak, living for life after dark at the bar. I taught them, just as I'd been taught, how to get a fake ID and how to be fashionably late but not miss the fun. They came down as often as possible. I suffered without them during the week and many weekends, but when the summer came all was well again.

Brian and Steve, of course, would also attend this event of events.

Bette revered adventure and fun. Or should I say drama? She could have you laughing until you peed your pants, but then things would go wrong and suddenly you're explaining yourself to a small-town cop in an ice storm. Some sort of drama always slashed its way into her life. She told bold lies and just assumed we were all stupid enough to believe them. The funny thing is, not one of us ever believed her tall tales of inheritance, evil relatives kidnapping her, and exotic island ownership; but because Bette never got this, she worked really hard at keeping the tales going. We'd have liked her without the idea of money coming into the group soon, or the possibility of island takeovers. Matter of fact, we were friends with her despite her lies, not because of them—but she couldn't see this.

During our freshman year Bette fell in love with Ranelle and they got their own trailer. I would lie on the trailer's floor and read their copy of *The Joy of Lesbian Sex* while pondering my own sexuality. I thought I was for sure bi because I was in love with Boy George. I mean, he is a *guy*. Besides, I couldn't really be a lesbian. Didn't pussy taste and smell bad? The only reason I thought I might like women is because Ranelle told me I was most likely gay. She couldn't believe I hadn't had sex with a guy yet and didn't seem to care about it. When I blamed my virginity on my Christian values, she looked at me and said, "Yeah, that's what I used to say."

I looked at her, dumbfounded, but didn't respond with what I was thinking, which was: *Really?? Did you really fervently believe that you were perfectly Christian, righteously so, spiritually straining to do, think, pray every right action, thought, and prayer? Ranelle, did you plot and plan your passion instead of just falling into the arms of any drunk college freshman that grabbed for you? Did you really believe you were a virgin on purpose, waiting for real love so you could tell it to Jesus in a prayer and he'd understand and say, "I will tell Our Father that marriage isn't the right sacrifice but love is. Love is, Sharlene, and he will understand your sacrifices"?*

What if my mind had tricked me? What if my mind or even God or my newly discovered Goddess had known that I couldn't handle being gay but didn't want me dirtied by heterosexuality and had saved me as a pure being until I was ready for the truth? Was that possible?

The only make-out sessions I'd had in all of two years were with effeminate gay men who also told me I was gay. And then there was the fact that I got crushed out on certain female classmates and would write lengthy journal entries about them. Bette and Ranelle both thought I wanted Ranelle, but that wasn't really true. I just liked her being older and wiser (all of five years) and acting protective of me.

Anyway, Bette and Ranelle exchanged vows and the party got started. Vanessa, Blanche, China, and Chloe had their court running to and fro taking care of the hors d'oeuvres and the preparation of the cake. The queens themselves did no running for anything, but they did run the show. Vodka, tequila, gin, and—most important—La Donna's secret-ingredient punch flowed, so much so that I barely remember anything that happened after the vows and before Shani.

I noticed this cute blond who looked like the lead singer of Wilson Phillips. She seemed to be my age and appeared to be single. Miracle. (I later found out that it was indeed too good to be true; she was not single.) She had long bangs over to one side, naturally cute—not much makeup, yet definitely femme.

I was way too shy to approach her on my own. I had no experience with women, except to have happily received a compliment or two. I remember the first time a woman gave me a clit surge (that I was conscious of). The guys and I had been out dancing when I met these two cute young dykes in from out of town—friends of our friend Troy. They were such a hot couple on the dance floor, I couldn't help but notice them, and they turned out to be the first out lesbian couple I actually talked to. (This was before I hung out with Bette and Ranelle.) Troy introduced us; he went, "They're lezzzies," stuck out his tongue, laughed, and said, "Shar's probably a lezzie, she just doesn't know it yet." They shook my hand, then we all went into our own grooves, hitting the bar and dance floor. They didn't pay me much mind, or so I thought. Later that night Troy and I squished onto my twin dorm bed and his dyke friends sandwiched onto the other. As I collapsed on the bed still in my micro-miniskirt—a light-and-dark-blue-striped denim one that zipped to my waist on each side—I surreptitiously pulled my zipper up to reveal plenty of thigh as I lay on my belly. One of the girls said, "My girlfriend likes your skirt," and the other said, "Yeah, we noticed your ass on the dance floor. You've got the best ass."

A hot current as distinct as a hand itself ran up the insides of my thighs, under that tiny skirt, and over my pussy to circle my clit. A compliment from a lesbian turned me on—*and I got a compliment about my ass!* "Thank you," I said. We lay in the almost dark with a plane of light streaming in under the dorm room door. I listened to them fuck and to Troy snore. I couldn't move and I couldn't sleep. *I think I'm a lesbian* ran over and over again in my head.

So that was the extent of my lesbian interactions except for Bette and Ranelle. Really, I didn't get *too* worked up over the sporty blond I'd spotted at the wedding, because she didn't even seem a possibility. Not because she was "out of my league" or any such nonsense but because how do you start *doing* that? I mean, it's like the difference between watching bumper cars on the sidelines and suddenly being strapped in behind the wheel. How do you get there? Well, I didn't know, so I just did what I always did: I hung out with the fags and queens and had a blast.

But as we laughed and partied, the girl got closer and closer to the perimeter of my group. When I went to get into the bathroom line along the trailer's hallway, she followed me.

"Hi," she giggled. Yes, giggled. We were all of 18. She also was spilling her spiked punch. "I'm sorry. You're cute."

Then her mouth was on me and we kissed sloppily, falling into the bathroom.

"Girl, take that fish somewhere else!" La Donna screeched, leaning up from a line of coke on the mascara-and Clairol-stained counter. "This is not your fishin' pond. Heeeelll. Heh-heh." She laughed at herself, and the others by the toilet laughed, too. They pushed us out the door.

"No pussy-lickin' in here, you little carpet-munchin tramps!"

We didn't stop kissing as they pushed us back into the hall. She tasted great. I couldn't believe it. Some girl was kissing me, making me really a lesbian. My nipples sparked with mini-explosions. My hands held her firmly, pressing into the small of her back. But we kept falling. Very drunk, not stable, but fun, fun, fun. I finally squirmed upright and pulled myself away.

"I gotta pee." I pounded on the flimsy door.

She smiled sweetly, looked into my eyes like she was asking for something, then twirled her hand into mine, weaving her fingers between my fingers, pulling me like we were girls in a movie going to a secret hiding place. Soon there would surely be flowers floating around our heads. "There are plenty of places to pee around here. We'll go outside." She looked over her shoulder and smiled again to be sure I wasn't struggling any more than necessary to get out of the tiny hallway.

We tripped down the three black metal stairs and ran out behind the garden.

"I can't pee if you watch," I said.

"OK, OK..." She turned her back, crossed her arms in front of her, stood guard for me. Then she peed, too. Then we went to the punch table and started making out again.

"Honey bun, I am sorry to do this to ya, but we gotta leave pretty soon." Brian's voice appeared from nowhere.

Kissing, kissing...I ignored him.

"Brian's mom is gonna figure out what's going on if we don't get the car back. C'mon, mama, you're finishin' up," Steve said into my other ear.

Brian had originally asked his mom if we could go down

to a special event and spend the night. "Absolutely not," she'd told him. So much for telling the truth. We'd then made something up and driven the 90 miles to Carbondale at high speeds anyway.

"Nooooo, c'mon," I stressed, pulling away from her delicious mouth. My first lesbian mouth.

"I'm sorry." Brian was sorry, but he didn't understand. I could not leave!

"Thirty more minutes," I said.

"No, Sharlene, we have to go."

"Thirty, please, please, pleeeaaassse."

"Ten."

Shani made these seductive kitten eyes at me. Wow, that worked. Hook, line, and sinker. I felt like Bugs Bunny when he gets hypnotized and his feet float up and he follows the girl bunny. She whispered, "You can't leave," all drunk and happy. "Let's hide." She laughed again, then we ran away to fall behind the propane tank on the edge of the yard.

Once horizontal, we pushed our hands up each other's shirts. Oh, God, oh, God, I knew my nipples were sensitive, but this blond drove me crazy. Every touch made my crotch burn and ache. My nipples tingled with such electricity I thought I would shock her fingers. Her skin, her hair, her *girliness* consumed me. Lesbianism rocked. This is what girls, women, taste like, feel like, smell like? Little blond neck fuzz soft on my lips before I sank my teeth into her skin, breasts curving into my hands and filling my mouth, and just the warm feel of our bare bellies against each other. Her shirt came off and mine had no back, leaving everything under it easily accessed (sooner or later I lost it anyway). I unzipped her skirt and stretched my fingers past her belly button. Her tan skin was interrupted by small thin panties. I gasped. This turned me on even more. Each moment seemed to prove that my body could go to yet a new level of excitement and desire. Every second I thought I would explode, yet I lived to experience every next second that was better than the one before it. Panties. Panties cover tickliness, cover nastiness, cover girl parts, cover pussy. Oh, this was so nasty and slutty and fantastic. I shoved my hand into the place I had only visited on myself. Ah, warm, moist, delicate, tickly on my fingertips. She gasped and arched her back and yanked her shorts down farther.

"Can I...do this?"

"Yes, yes," she moaned and quickly grabbed my head to pull me into another passionate kiss. I think my lip bled. I rubbed her clit just a little, but from her squirming I instinctively knew to separate the pink lips of her pussy and press my finger in between. I went in. It felt so natural. She gasped happily and ground against me. I didn't know if I was doing anything right, but if I wasn't she fixed it by moving with me to make it right. I went in and out as best as I could, then easily slipped another finger into her. "Oh, God, yes," she moaned. I loved how hot and slickery she felt around my fingers. We were connected. I fucked her and kissed her and pinched and pulled at her nipple. She raised her knee, pushing up my skirt, and smashed her thigh into me. I ground my hips as we kept kissing. Her hand reached down the back of my skirt and pressed against my asshole. She didn't go in, just pressed in a circle. To be honest, it was all so fast, at one point we were just pushing and grabbing at any piece of girl we could get.

"Lezzzbianss separate! I command thee!" Blanche's scratchy voice ripped into our paradise. Brian must have gotten back-up. "We are approaching the pussy propane tank. Please buckle your belts and put your pussy away," she keened like a stewardess directed by God. "There ya go, darlin', I warned 'em for ya," she told Brian, then hobbled away. Brian carefully peered around the tank, a young fag fearful of what he might see. Then Steve just bounded up, no worries.

"Shar! We've got to go." He was getting that tense tone we all get if we know we're gonna be in trouble.

"Noooo," I groaned, but smiled at Shani under me. I couldn't help the ear-to-ear grin that dominated my face.

"Mama, I'm sorry to do this," Steve said to me; then to Brian he said, "You got the other arm?"

"Yep." They pulled me off her and stood me up.

Brian laughed. "Girlfriend, you're a mess." He pulled my skirt down. "Get your shirt."

The gray tie was still around my neck. I bent over to fetch my shirt, which was smashed up under the smelly silver-painted steel, and fell back onto Shani for more rubbing.

"Noooo!" they said in unison. Brian grabbed me and Steve got my shirt.

"Can't I get her number at least?" I pleaded.

"You already hid for an hour, we're going." Brian led my stumbling, drunken legs, half holding me up. Shani ran up to our car as the boys stuffed me in the backseat. She kissed me again and gave me her number.

I collapsed in the back seat, giggly and higher than Dolly Parton's hair. I couldn't believe how fantastic my whole body and mind felt. I really was so high. After a few minutes of mooning in the backseat over my hour with Shani, I lay there with my fist curled up to my face like a child. Suddenly, I smelled my fingers. "Oh," I inhaled. She wasn't gone. I had her here. Talk about a "lightbulb moment." My eyes widened as I stared at my fingers. I tried to focus on them and see if I could see her. Not much but the smell. I closed my eyes and inhaled slowly and deeply. My head swooned. This was too much. I inhaled over and over again, until I became lightheaded. I truly thought I'd gone to heaven for a few minutes.

"Smell my fingers! Smell my fingers!" I exclaimed, thrilled with this new discovery. I shoved my hands over the seat and into the boys' faces. They squirmed and shooed me away, making dramatic icky faces until we all laughed.

I kept saying it almost the whole way home, "Sssmell my fingurrrrs." I was for real. I wanted them to know how trippy this was, and I was way too drunk with punch and lust to take their "no"s seriously. Before we got home Brian spun into a gas station and jerked to stop at the water and air area. "Here ya go."

"What?"

"You better wash those hands before we get home."

I crawled out of the car and washed them, then happily discovered that the smell of her still lingered.